COME OUT TO PLAY

COME OUT TO PLAY

By Alex Comfort

Crown Publishers, Inc. New York

Library of Congress Cataloging in Publication Data

Comfort, Alexander, 1920-
  Come out to play.

  I. Title.
PZ3.C7337Co3 [PR6005.0388]   823'.9'12   75-2008
ISBN 0-517-52147-4

FOR JANE
Who fixed all this

Contents

Publisher's Note

In 1961 Dr. Alex Comfort, combining wit, comedy, science, satire, and innovative imagination, created a novel. Not an ordinary novel. A novel of which the *London Daily Telegraph* said, ". . . unremittingly amusing, and the ideas it throws out are not to be dismissed as scientific nonsense"—an evaluation that hit the target as accurately as our author did in his prediction of things to come. For, not long after this imaginative flight, the first sex clinic was founded by Masters and Johnson, followed by many others of similar nature. All could have been patterned after the pioneer effort of Dr. George Goggins and Dulcinea McGredy. None ever will or could match the wit and charm and fun and good humor exercised by these fictional prototypes.

The introduction of so revolutionary a concept was not enough for the fertile creativity of the author. His deep involvement in science had to find expression here too, and it did with the discovery of the world's most effective aphrodisiac. Once again the *Daily Telegraph* was prophetic: *The New York Times* on December 24, 1974, printed a long article under the headline "Sex Attractant Chemicals from Women Isolated." True, this is only an early stage in the development of an aphrodisiac such as Comfort describes, possibly never to be achieved in fact. Yet, here is further proof of how soundly based his imaginative flights are.

Alex Comfort, medical biologist, foremost expert on human sexuality, world-famous authority on aging, who brought fun into the teaching of sexual techniques with his revolutionary *Joy of Sex*, commented, "*Come Out to Play* started to be simply a comic novel. I think now it was the manifesto of which *The Joy of Sex* commences the implementation." When we learned that only the British reading public had had the opportunity to enjoy this product of Comfort's genius, we decided to make *Come Out to Play* available to American readers, and we heartily commend it to you for hours of pure enjoyment.

Author's Note

The story of this book is possibly funnier than the book itself, and a warning against writing humorous novels. Not only did I cast Dr. George Goggins for the role of Super-Cad and find that everyone, from the girl who typed the manuscript on, took him for a self-portrait: I recounted the plot to Dulcinea the first time I dated her seriously, and we two have been fated, *mutatis mutandis,* to act a fair amount of it out. Even the science fiction has caught up with us, in that human pheromones are now a serious possibility—so much so that a lot of the literature research which went into COTP ended up as a review in *Nature*. You can judge how far in antiquity this story, which now reads like current affairs, was written by the fact that in those days explicit sexual matters had to be written in Sanskrit and it wasn't done to treat the Friworld, its clowns, its spies, and its vermin generally, with disrespect. When they do the CIA, they'll probably flush out the goons who were after Marcel and his 3-blindmycin. I'm not so much arrogant at the anticipation as a little scared by the power of would-be comedy to expose plans I didn't know I had, but no matter—Long Live Goggins and Dulcinea, and may their orgasms and their *chutzpah* never grow less.

Alex Comfort

1
THE OWL AND
THE PUSSY-CAT

"FROM THIS HOOK," SAID THE GUIDE, "WAS SUS-
pended the iron cage, two and a half meters square, in which
Cardinal Balue was imprisoned for eleven years by Louis XI.
He had, however, little ground for complaint, as the cage was
his own invention."

We stood and looked at the hook, at the two bare lamp
bulbs which illuminated it, and at the names of visiting Americans scratched on the walls. The place smelled of mushrooms.

"We will now reascend the stairs," said the guide, "and
see the cell where Sforza was kept in perpetual reclusion."

Unfortunately, the guide was a professional funny man.
In Sforza's cell he turned out the lights without warning to
give the ladies the feel of the place, said he hoped that the
gentlemen would not abuse the opportunity, and snickered.
I was getting tired of him, of standing while he was funny, and

of keeping near the front of the party (a pointless excursion is much more pointless if you can't see), and I was under perpetual pressure from a small dense man with an eyeshade, baseball fashion, and a shiny camera. What looked like fat on him must have been partly muscle, for when he pushed he was as hard as a brick, front and back. His breathing was audible; sometimes it was actually vocalized, as "excuse, excuse, excuse," sometimes it was a natural wheezing which evidently meant the same. The camera sticking into my side looked like a Zeiss but was actually a Russian Kiev, and I wondered where he'd got it from.

The tomb of Agnes Sorel was in a little room that would not hold us all, and I let him go ahead of me to pay his respects to her—moved out of the chapel on moral grounds by her rivals, and given a new pair of hands with a prayer book in them to symbolize the penitence she probably never experienced—he could say "excuse, excuse, excuse" to her, and it might cheer her. The girl I was watching, meanwhile, had sat down on the parapet, with her handbag beside her, holding her forehead with both hands, and looking, by now, really unwell. She hadn't looked too fit when Eyeshade helped her on the bus, and obviously the headache, or the period, or whatever it was was getting worse. I didn't mind Eyeshade pushing, since I am long and he is short, but at each castle I was coming to resent him more. He had paid his money and was going to see castles to the bitter end—she trotted after him, leaning against walls while the guide was funny, sitting when she could. Eyeshade bustled back periodically to be solicitous, but never in the least inclined to take her back to the bus or buy her some strong coffee. On some of these visits he made her bend forward and rubbed the back of her neck, but that was all: after each motion of solicitude he was back again like a cock parrakeet, running up and down his perch, excuse-excusing and photographing the lead waterspouts, which are unique at Loches.

She was thin, nicely dressed, high heels, big handbag, big knobby ring on her wedding finger, hair that had been dyed, or bleached, and was growing out at the roots. Her girdle was too tight and flattened her—one wondered why, because under her clothes she was clearly firm enough without it—hard, perhaps, in the same way that Eyeshade was hard. They couldn't be husband and wife, I felt certain—boss and secretary, daddy and mistress, possibly both; not English, French, or American —West German, perhaps, at a first guess, but when Eyeshade and she talked it sounded like Hungarian. Her perfume had a narcissus base that went with her shape—I could tell it was hers without checking the others—it had quietly filled first the bus then Cardinal Balue's cell. Outside Agnes Sorel's tomb, she was rubbing her hands against her forehead, getting paler and paler. Eyeshade was inside. Nobody else took any notice of her—they were hanging over the battlements with a guidebook, identifying buildings down below.

I offered her an aspirin.

"No, really, thank you," she said, in English to my French —not English English, but something very, very close to it. "It's only a headache, and mine always go by midday."

"You're sure you're all right?" I asked her.

"Thank you. My husband's a doctor." Not a brush-off, this, simply a fact, and she looked thoroughly grateful. I was thinking that Eyeshade was one down for our profession when "excuse-excuse" came up behind me and he was there. "This gentleman was just asking if I'd like an aspirin," she said. "My husband." We bowed, and they both thanked me again, he as genuinely as she, and that was that. A few minutes later she was still sitting, but Eyeshade was sitting slantwise beside her and working really hard on her cervical vertebrae with his thumbs. This was a load off my mind, for the sake of the profession, because it was evident from the timbre of his performance that he was not a doctor but an osteopath. Paddling in her neck, said something behind me, with his damned fingers.

After that we broke into two parties and came down from the castle separately. I passed Eyeshade and the girl at the stand that sold iron jewelry. She was holding his arm: for the time being at least the osteopathy seemed to have worked.

While the rest went off to find set meals, I bought a half pound of Roquefort, which I hadn't had for three whole years, butter, and a loaf, and settled down on a public bench by the river, in sight of the bus. Twenty minutes later I saw that Eyeshade and the girl were four benches down, behind me. Evidently in that time they'd dined as much as they intended, probably on raw cabbage and nuts. He had a newspaper, she had the Blue Guide. They were reading side by side. Half an hour later, when I got up, she had the Blue Guide in her hand, but she wasn't reading—simply staring ahead. Eyeshade was stretched along the bench asleep with his head in her lap and the paper over his face. The girl had her other hand under it, on his forehead, smoothing it across and across—her fingers carried more conviction that his had done. Still she didn't look married.

I still don't know why I did it—they might have been devoted to each other. When I caught her eye, quite solemn, recognizing, but with nothing in it but emptiness, I made a pantomime gesture of taking Eyeshade by the two ends and chucking him in the river. She looked back steadily, then down at him lying on her, then back at me. She wasn't angry. She started to smile, but the smile began and regressed again like a door which part-opens and then shuts. All the time she never stopped smoothing and smoothing at Eyeshade's forehead.

In the lounge at Tours, Eyeshade bustled up as if he'd come on purpose. He was definitely friendly. "Is to thank you once over for you think to give pills to my wife," he said. "Very kind. Ectually"—just right—"in my house we never use pills, is poison, you know, but this was nice of you. My card."

The card said Dr. (Herb.) Zimbalist, Otto: Chiropractor: no address, no telephone number. Its owner said, "You going far?"

"I'm doing three days of châteaux from Tours," I said, "then I've got to get back to Paris."

* 4

"Us too, the three days of castles. These I like, and my wife, when she is well."

He sat down by me.

"Now I see, you were today eating cheese. Is the real medicine. That too I like."

"And your wife?" I asked.

"My wife—no. Not as I." It seemed to disappoint him that she didn't.

"You think if she ate enough cheese she wouldn't suffer from headaches?" I said. He seemed as if he'd take me seriously whatever I said.

"Is possible. No, I think not. That is the neck." He rubbed his own. "Is here, the bones. I tell you something, she is funny —I have offered, but she does not like I replace them. Rub, yes—replace radically, is better—no."

He looked me over as if he were planning to sell me something and wondered if I'd buy it, while I wondered what it was going to be. I expected him to continue, "Is good for your neck too. Fee also moderate."

"Is Dulcinea," Otto said, "pretty name."

For a moment I'd thought that it was his wife he was going to sell me. It had sounded infernally like it. There was a confidential, propositional glaze on his eye which I thought I recognized from very different surroundings.

"I luff her!" Otto went on. Evidently not, then. In any event, I'd no intention of buying her—even if the next proposition was "is good for bed"—I could see that for myself, but I'd nowhere to put her.

"I luff her," said Otto. "We see you—good-bye." And he went very courteously and with a little waistless bow. I hoped he wasn't a mind reader as well as a bonesetter, because I'd misjudged him.

Otto was asleep on the seat ahead. When he slept, his breathing kept up "excuse-excuse," less clearly articulated than when he was awake, but still quite intelligible, and Dulcinea was sitting next me. They'd come down to the bus late, when only singles were left: Otto had brushed aside my offer to move and let them sit together. It crossed my mind again that he'd fixed this. However, if that was the way he wanted it, I had no objection. When he was asleep I changed places to give her the window. We were going through a forest of pear trees, with every pear in a little paper loincloth to protect it from birds. Harmless conversation had dried up. There seemed to be something intangible wrong with it; it didn't take hold, but tinkled. We hadn't spoken for several kilometers.

"You don't," I said, getting ready to duck, "*look* married to him."

She didn't lash out, but looked the answer without saying it. I found myself thinking "so that's all right"—then wondering why, because she didn't belong to me in any case. But at least we were talking normally now.

"I *am* married to him." She bridled a little. She's contradicted herself, I thought; what's she up to?

"Are you really Irish?" I asked her.

"Irish?"

"It says McGredy on the tag of your vanity bag."

"I'm Hispano-Celtic. And I came from Hungary. Any more questions?"

I explained I wasn't being gratuitously impertinent—only I'd lived in Ireland for years and I wondered which part she came from.

"That," she said, "is something I don't know. Now I'll start on you. You're a doctor. What sort of doctor?"

"A medical biologist."

"What do they do?"

"Medical biology."

"I mean, ears, eyes, fevers. . . ?"

Ever since I started it, I've found that work on human sexual behavior has two important social drawbacks. The first is that if you tell a woman exactly what you are working on (even if she is an intellectual) it is a definite overture, whether you like it or not, and women use "But what exactly do you *do?*" as a standard space-filler. The other is that people of both sexes, including those you least expect, infest you and hover. By hovering I mean that they hang about waiting for courage and opportunity to consult you without payment. You stimulate the kind of transference that attaches to the analyst, but with far less tendency to resistance.

"Oh, on fertility and so on," I told her.

For a moment she seemed to be on the verge of hovering. She might for all I knew be pining for a child—or dead scared she would have one. But this was a different kind of transference: she wanted to tell me, not pump me.

"My name is McGredy—actually it's Fuentes y McGredy, that's the Hispano-Celtic part—but it's a kind of accident. They knew father was Irish, but he was in—a hurry, and didn't actually leave his name."

I made a sympathy sound, but it wasn't wanted—she was as bright as ever; in fact she was telling it as a joke. Too bright, in fact. It must hurt, so I wouldn't laugh, even if she did.

"They'd got a rose called McGredy's Sunset, and that was Irish, so I was McGredy. Funny, isn't it?"

In that case she was lucky to have missed being called Maréchal Niel or President Hoover, but I didn't think this was the moment to say so.

"I was born in Buenos Aires. That's where they lived: later on it was Hungary, in Szeged."

I congratulated her on her English.

"I was at school," she said, "at Folkestone."

I agreed that Folkestone was a nice place.

"And now, even if you turn out my luggage, you won't find anything more that'll interest you. That," she said, "is positively all." She gave me a little toss of the head, for match point.

"All except Otto."

She'd been laughing when she took the slap at my inquisitiveness, though the laugh had a hard tip to it. But when I asked that, the whole thing changed—there was a momentary glimpse of a desolate little girl that made me really sorry I'd said it. I saw her pick herself up again almost instantly. She must have picked herself up a great many times.

"My husband has been very, very good to me—he got me out of Hungary. He didn't have to leave himself. He took a big risk for me and now he can't go back. That makes us both refugees."

She was already an expert at dodging that word "grateful." Until Otto woke up we talked unconvincingly about castle architecture, but two other people seemed to be continuing our real conversation just out of earshot, while we filled in time.

"Yes," said Otto, as his first eye opened, "is very educated in history and decoration, my wife. Better I think than buying all these guidebooks," and the smile they gave each other was genuine enough. The bus had been sufficiently noisy for me to be certain that he couldn't have overheard us, without special equipment. They went off at Chenonceaux, hand in hand. I saw them photographing each other with the château as background. I still couldn't explain to myself how we'd ever embarked on the conversation in the bus. It had peculiar features. I wouldn't have time to put my finger on them, however, for I wasn't due to spend another night at Tours. I'd booked a hotel in Paris that night, and I would have to drive back there after dinner. Otto and his wife didn't really matter, except for the theoretical interest of the thing—I would have liked to have known what our minds had been doing behind our backs.

It came to a head before that, however. On the bus I'd told them I was leaving. There was the usual "we'll swop addresses when we get back" routine, which nobody ever follows up. At dinner they nodded to me from their table; it was too far off across waiters and hors-d'oeuvre-loaded trolleys for conversation. I saw Otto taking the elevator in his socks, carrying his shoes in his hand.

I paid, surrendered the key, packed the car—in fact I'd gone, and there was no reason for me to come back into the hotel foyer; but I did so.

She came out of the elevator as I crossed the carpet to the door—looking for someone, possibly even for Otto, possibly for me. Whichever she'd expected, she saw me.

I ask you to believe that what happened was fully automatic—and that she seemed to be expecting it, or hoping for it, or afraid I wouldn't read the signals. Anyhow, the significant part of the transaction was all quite unspoken. When we did speak we were only verbalizing a concluded bargain, as a formality.

"I'm off now to Paris."

"Yes."

"You wouldn't like to come with me?"

"Yes."

"Get your things, quick. I'll bring the car round to the front."

"No, wait for me here. I'd rather go out with you."

Accordingly we never went back to the front of the hotel. She hurried down carrying something, we went through into the yard, and blundered in the dark of the garage until I could turn on the car lights. Helping her in I got a hand on her waist for the first time. We drove straight out of the yard, down the avenue by the station, and off. Dulcinea sat bolt upright, and the shadow of each plane tree flashed across her face. It never even occurred to me to make sure she hadn't pinched half of Dr. Otto's property to take with us.

All the pebble banks in the Loire were shining as we went over the bridge. The town lights stopped. We were now shut in together inside the same, personal skin—we might have been in space.

After a while she said, "You are a real doctor, aren't you?"

I told her I wasn't an imitation.

"No—I mean real; not like him. I thought you said you were a biologist."

I told her I was both.

"But if you're a real doctor, I'll get you into trouble."

I told her I thought I was more likely to get her into

trouble, when it came to that, and in any case she wasn't my patient, which was what mattered from the disciplinary point of view.

"You gave me an aspirin," she said.

"Fortunately you didn't take it."

We did Paris to Tours in four hours. Part of the way we sang a little—she told me I was a baritone, which was a new way of putting it. It was getting to morning, but still dark, when the night porter saw us in. Since I'd made this booking for myself only, there was no need for the argument over rooms, and Dulcinea didn't argue. She took her *fiche* away from me and filled it in herself. I didn't even trouble to see what she had put on it, though I remember making a mental note that I must get hold of it in the morning to copy down the date of her birthday.

The lift was very slow, small as a coffin, and the bulb had failed, so that it was quite dark inside, except when the floors went by, one after another, with glow lamps. It was like being in bed together already: we talked in a pillow whisper. I was pressed against Dulcinea, trying to keep my elbows off the control buttons.

"There are three questions one asks at about this stage," I said, in her ear, "but I needn't ask you the first."

"Am I a virgin?"

"Yes."

"No, but you could pretend it was yes to make sure. What's the other question?"

"Tough or tender?"

"Tough, please."

"One lump or two?"

"One and a half."

"The Moroccan bride," I whispered, "makes her man ravish her even if she loves him—it's supposed to be lucky."

"Yes."

"But he's got the *uzir* to help him."

"What's an uzir?"

"The best man—to sit on her head if she struggles."

"I expect we'll manage," said Dulcinea, "I'm nicer not sat on. Let's make it one lump only this time."

"Leaving one more fundamental question."

"Yes?"

"Everything storkproof?"

"Tactful! Yes, everything."

That, I thought, is the acid test that she knows her own mind.

"What did you put on your *fiche?*" I asked, as we stopped.

"My name—what did you expect?"

"Your real name?"

"Why not?"

"Well, for one thing, because you don't know mine."

"Tomorrow," she said. We'd covered the few feet of dowdy corridor. Dulcinea had the key. It was she who opened the door. The light in the bedroom didn't work either, it was hot and full of patchouli—I stopped only to get the windows open and the Venetian blind down for morning.

Undressing her I couldn't help wondering what the ancient Hindus would have called her: she was intermediate—more Lehmbruck than Maillol, not a lotus woman but possibly a seashell woman, though that typology isn't really appropriate to Europeans. "It makes a difference," I explained.

"Don't be informative, love me," she said.

When we got to grips she struggled so sincerely that I thought I must have hurt her and let go. "Call the best man!" she whispered. So I took hold again.

In most ways she was perfect, in fact it wasn't for days that I realized how odd her perfection was, coming to hand naturally with tricks like the *tour de France* which I wouldn't have expected her to know, but not knowing others which I would have thought she couldn't have missed, even from Dr. Otto. Also, we had to adjust.

"Was that good?" I asked her.

"Lovely, lovely, lovely."

"Yes," I said, "it's the perfect release of tension."

The result was so spectacular that I thought I must have

got her hair caught in my watch strap. She let out a screech that had nothing at all to do with pleasure and banged on my chest with both fists.

"Shut up! Why did you have to say that? Damn you! Damn your beastly, cold, therapeutic approach—it's hateful!"

I turned her over quickly and reverted to something I wasn't so likely to misjudge, but for a full minute there was no result. Then she began laughing, and the laughs became mixed with reassuring gasps—I remember thinking that the Indian sages hadn't thought of that one, and so much for the Brahminic mania for classification. Even when she had finished the laughs kept erupting like groups of bubbles.

"All right now?" I said.

"Yes. But it's so funny."

"What is?"

"Being loved by a biologist."

I told her it would be very much worse next time, because I'd left my notebook in my trousers when I got into bed, instead of having it strapped round my waist.

She stretched and put her head on me, rubbing with her hair.

"I'll get used to it. I think I like it. I'll make the notes," she said. "But it's still funny. You're so detached."

I asked her, what did she expect, since this was something I took seriously—if you want to dance a demonstration quick-step with a new partner, or even an old one, you didn't just rely on Terpsichore and go at it as a romp: someone had to know the sequence and think where he was putting his feet. "By tradition it's the man going forward and the woman going backward—dancing, I mean: it's much the same with this."

"But I always thought *this* came naturally," she said.

"And most people can dance naturally after a fashion: it pleases them, but it doesn't win prizes. Moreover if she has some idea of the steps the girl can follow, but the man's got to keep intoning 'corté—outside spin—hesitation—quick six—fishtail—' in his own ear, or they'll both be sitting on their dignities in the middle of the dance floor. When I upset you then, I started to spin the wrong way."

She was laughing so hard that her ear was making my chest sore, and stuffing the sheet into her mouth.

"Anyhow," I said, "I got the impression that the performance justified the method."

"Go to sleep! You talk too much."

This is true, so I settled down.

"And thank you for being so relaxed about it," she said, after a few minutes.

That was our last word till breakfast time.

I left Dulcinea in one of the big Paris stores. She was going shopping. I was going to see Boyo.

I love department stores. If temples are the indices of Hindu culture, stores are the temples of ours—our religious iconography spends all its energy on the celebration of death and barrenness, so that the celebration of the good things of life has been driven into the department store, where it pays somebody to celebrate them. The ethics of the profit motive still don't stop me from enjoying these places. This one had a Shelleyan stained-glass cupola, propped on tall steel trees that bore everything—colored fabrics, drinks, perfumes, tools, music-and-literature insofar as they were portable and salable: from the galleries up in the metal branches you could look down into a slow whirlpool of women and girls, or join it and go into the paradisal forest which was built into our nervous systems when we were a food-gathering species and nothing had to be paid for, under long creepers of printed fabrics and through clumps of petticoats, cheeses, and stationery:

> the excellent trees have divine smell, taste and touch, yield everything desired, and give all kinds of apparel, jewels decorated with pearls and gems befitting both men and women and suitable to all seasons, these the noble trees yield; and here other trees produce bed-steads with fine coverlets and garlands that gladden the

heart, expensive foods and drinks, and damsels noted for their excellent character, beauty and youth . . .

in other words, the lot. The Ramayana didn't have a department store in mind, but hits it beautifully; even though the girls of excellent character don't count openly as merchandise in our culture, they were there too if you kept your eyes open.

I couldn't resist stopping on the gallery to look down into all this, and watch Dulcinea from above—one view I hadn't had —as she went through the middle of the whirlpool: then I walked round the forest a bit, simply looking and enjoying the colors. Accordingly, I still had the jungle analogy in mind when I got to Boyo's office. It turned out to be appropriate.

I hadn't seen Jebb Jollyboy for ten years. He wasn't a man I liked though one had to give him the sort of grudging respect one gives to the fellow who gets away with it—you had to hand it to him, but you hoped that one day somebody would. When I first encountered his name he was listed with me to share the dissection of the same thorax. We moved together after that and should have qualified together. Unfortunately Boyo didn't qualify. Having failed to do so he passed out of my life, to be publicity agent to a firm of druggists. I'd seen him once and once only since, at the medical exhibition, looking like a specialist, but yielding, bending slightly in the middle for downtrodden GPs to step over him—when I saw the brillance of this performance I knew I should hear more of Boyo. He could have stayed writing circulars indefinitely, but if he knew nothing else he knew the game (unfortunately it isn't a subject in finals), and he knew how to wait. Boyo got himself made personal publicity adviser to Crutworthy, a jumped-up evening-class lecturer who had just become Leader of the Opposition. This was a tough, grubby, unremunerative job. Neither the public nor the other Labour leaders had to know that Boyo existed. He, for his part, had to see that articles praising Crutworthy got into the Conservative press, organize fake opinion polls in which Crutworthy was scored for qualities such as Leadership and Integrity, leak real or imaginary party discussions discreditable to Crutworthy's rivals, and see that C. himself was sober when he broadcast. Above all, he had to build his man up as a Responsible Statesman Uncommitted to Rash Policies. The second half was easy, as Crutworthy wasn't committed to any policy but getting Crutworthy into office, but the first part was harder, because the great man insisted on introducing all the dirtiest tricks of minor academic politics into public life.

Anyhow, Boyo had done remarkably well. He not only got C. looking less like a rodent on television, but when it became obvious that, largely owing to the presence of C. in it, the Labour Party was going to be out for years, he managed to transport his principal, in one continuous movement, from Leader of the Party to Labour life peer and managing director of Rocket Rackets, Inc., without losing him one cheer from the party conference (Boyo did it by building up as an authority on space research, though neither of them knew a sputnik from an astrolabe, and within a year, C. was opening scientific conferences).

As leader of the Opposition, Crutworthy hadn't much money—he did it all, initially at least, from sheer love of the game—but Boyo was patient, and the investment turned out excellently. Lord Outfall of Barking, who was Crutworthy gone up, paid off handsomely, both for services rendered and as a precaution against memoirs. Boyo, however, had the sense to see that this wouldn't last, because by now there were other Crutworthies at the top of the Labour Party for public opinion to worry about, and in view of the shortness of memory even memoirs wouldn't matter to Lord Outfall for very long. Accordingly he persuaded his man to compound for the balance by getting him the Directorship of the new United Nations Office of Peace and Plenty. This was an organization devised originally by the State Department as a counter to FAO and WHO, which were being too neutral about the standards of living in Africa and had started distributing rice and medicine without any concomitant military bases; as its main aim in life was to talk in grandiose terms and see nobody did anything, it suited Boyo down to the ground. Under him it really lived up to its name. Boyo was currently keeping more intellectual layabouts in peace and plenty than any patron since Lorenzo de' Medici.

The essential feature of Boyo's career, then, apart from the initial setback over finals, which for once he couldn't fiddle, was that nothing he had ever done had been a failure so far as Boyo was concerned. The only possible exception was a brief spell with the British Council in Yugoslavia, and that was hardly Boyo's fault—he was not to know that his first name was a rude word in Serbo-Croat. When my second three-year term with the India government's population project was up, and I wanted to arrange a spell in Europe before renewing it, I had consulted Boyo—not because I respected him, but because I knew him. I wanted to work in Paris, because I'd already been offered a laboratory bench there at the Institute of Human Biology—Boyo was in Paris, and Boyo knew where one could get an income (the institute job wasn't paid).

Boyo's reply had come by cable: ALL BIG THREE ANXIOUS EMPLOY YOU CONSULTANT STOP RUSSIANS CONTRACEPTION AMERICANS DITTO BRITISH WILL WRITE STOP. Shortly after that I'd had a letter from the British Embassy in Paris requesting me, if I went there to agree to act as consultant in connection with an international conference, of medical importance, and contact Boyo on arrival. That made three, so I came.

I was now after Boyo's head, because on the night of my arrival in Paris, a full three months later, I got a second cable, sent the day before, which had been to Delhi and back, and said HOLD EVERYTHING STOP RED PARTY LINE BABIES CHANGED STOP CATHOLIC PRESIDENT ELECTED DITTO STOP DONT COME UNTIL SUMMONED STOP. By that time I had committed myself to three years' leave from my Indian work, put in a deputy to take over, accepted a bench at the institute, and come. Boyo, moreover, was taking a few days off. The excursion which had so unexpectedly given me Dulcinea was filling in time until he got back.

Boyo's office had been built specially. It was like a huge glass puzzle, cubical and transparent so that on all the floors one could see secretaries running about, plants growing, type-writers masticating paper, uniformed messengers inspecting their white gloves, and long lines of olive-colored tin cup-boards—pointless activity, like the running of balls and flashing of lights in a pin table, yet working overtime and full of honest people and pretty girls with lives of their own, busy under Boyo's pill-pushing direction, making nothing—except trouble for themselves, and their children, and their children's children. And yet not one of them burned the obscene place down. Artists had decorated it with murals—scores of crafts-men had put it up, and behind them all the technicians of a culture had concocted the plastics and the dyes and the pre-stressed members, and gardeners had raised the rubber plants and the monsteras to grow in the foyer. It was as full of live people as an Indian temple is of carving, and one could watch them at it from the street, but the dead figures on temples celebrate Life, or at least Release: these living figures were busy in their expensive, cultured, gracious-living-minded hive, celebrating missiles and monkey business and the imaginings of homicidal dwarfs generally. And on the air-conditioned top floor, with pictures by Raoul Dufy and Matisse and Bernard Buffet, and tapestries by Lurçat, and a pretty, cultured secre-tary, was Jebb Jollyboy, O.B.E., failed student turned para-site, translating their nasty devices and knavish tricks into fact and cash.

Like all these outposts of the Free World, it was the sort of place Heliogabalus would have built if he'd lost his potency and had the Museum of Modern Art behind him to compensate for it.

The chairs in Boyo's anteroom were wicker cat baskets on legs, intended for naked models to curl up in, which was prob-ably the association which made Boyo buy them. The place

* 17

was transparent, however, which must have cramped his style. I could see the Great Man coming several rooms away and, worse still, hear him. He was singing at the top of his voice.

"This will be Mr. Jebb-Jollyboy," said the belle at the desk, as if he and she and they were all usefully employed at the most reasonable job in the world—"I'll let him know at once that you're here, Dr. Goggins,"—though she could see as well as I could that Boyo was coming straight at me, still singing gibberish.

"With my Nato, skato, genocide and hate, O
Freedum, bleedum, phoney O!

"Sing a song of cynicism! Hallo, old boy—I expected you yesterday. You know you bloody radical, I'm coming to share your opinions: the latest thing is that we've got to put up the publicity to get bloody Franco the Nobel Peace Prize. No, honestly, I mean it—we've had it in writing. Washington has spoken. It cannot tell a lie—with its little chopper. How is the stock of whitewash, Miss Carr?"

"I'll leave you with Dr. Goggins, Mr. Jollyboy," said the belle. The performance was evidently normal. But nevertheless, I knew Boyo, and he wasn't usually as boisterous as this. His usual public act was obsequious efficiency, not the zany. I guessed he was bally well ashamed of himself for letting me down, and the display of hypomania was for my benefit.

"Well," said Boyo, "let's have a look at you. I've got you your job."

I told him he'd better have, after the promise he'd given me of three separate jobs.

"That was beyond my control—I ask you," said Boyo. "They did all want you when I wrote—it was they who let you down, not me. And I tried to stop you—if you'd been coming by air like someone really contemporary you'd have had my cable."

"Well, what have you got?" I said. "I won't say any more

about the others, but the surviving job had better be good. I have to live and I have responsibilities."

"It's an advisory thing—technical expert—look, first of all, I've got to tell you it's confidential, of course. All right?"

"Which means it's crooked?"

"Not in the least—after all, you haven't taken it yet: I'd have thought that was a perfectly normal proviso. Agreed, so I can go ahead?"

"Agreed. Provisionally," I said.

"Well, what it comes to is this. They've got a document."

"Who have?"

"Her Britannic Majesty's whatnot—actually, of course, that means the Americans. But the kingpin you have to deal with is Fossil-Fundament—you know, the Foreign Secretary— I don't know if you've kept up with home affairs: even I can't remember all these blokes' names, and I deal with them."

I told him that I knew all about Fossil-Fundament, and that if I remembered, the only scientific advisers he was likely to need would be an entomologist or a pest-control officer to spray him with the appropriate chemical.

"I know, I know—but hold on till you've heard about it. He's got a document to present to the United Nations Committee on Nuclear Tests, and he wants an independent opinion from a fertility man. The Communists are telling all the black men that nuclear tests will make monkeys of them—brass monkeys—and we've got to combat that."

"We have? Fundament has."

"Well, for official purposes I am the voice of Fundament."

I was beginning to feel a sinking motion in Boyo's orange, fitted carpet: if this was Boyo's job for me, I was going to have to support Dulcinea and a year's work from my earnings as a street musician, and I told him so, leaving out Dulcinea.

"But why? He wants an independent expert to comment on a report—that's all—and probably testify before the UN. And he's willing to put that same expert in charge of a short series of tests—I don't know what that will be in cash, but it won't be stingy, and he told me specifically that the whole job would rate a decoration."

"Do I look like a knight?" I said.

"No, but you could look like an O.B.E.—we'll be delighted to have you."

"An independent expert," I said, "means an expert who isn't getting several thou and an O.B.E. That would be a dependent expert, wouldn't it? And an independent expert has a free hand."

"Of course you'd have a free hand."

"To say the whole thing's a swindle if it is one?"

"Well, nominally, yes."

"And in fact?"

"Well, look—they aren't going to hire an independent expert to comment on a report if he isn't going to endorse it, are they? This fallout thing is dicey for them politically—you know that as well as I do. But if you endorse it—in general terms, that is, you can be as independent as you like afterward."

I waited for him to go on. It suddenly clicked why Boyo was so keen to get me in—why, in fact, he tried this one on me at all. He couldn't get an expert, because nobody would touch it. And he was getting desperate; Fundament must be in trouble too.

"Look," said Boyo—I was looking—"You know I respect your opinions. But try the thing—you needn't be enthusiastic about it, I'm sure—wait till you see it: it doesn't seem to me to say very much at all. All they want you to do is not disagree with it in a bloodyminded way, you follow? I'm sure if you can accept that you're on. You seem to be assuming . . ."

I still waited for him. "As a matter of fact," said Boyo, "this report is dead, frozen secret, but I've got it here—I'll show it to you, so that you can see it's harmless. But for Christ's sake don't tell anyone you've seen it. Can I rely on your discretion?"

That wasn't a Boyo phrase—probably a Fundamentalism. I told him I relied on it myself, so I didn't see why he shouldn't.

Boyo buzzed and called for the file as if it were St. Peter's nightshirt. The blonde brought it in a sort of reliquary. Boyo waited till the servants had left before handing it to me. "Now, I'm putting myself in your hands, you know," he said. I read it from end to end without speaking, while Boyo tapped on his teeth with a paperknife. I handed it back to him with suitable reverence.

"Thank you," I said.

"Well—fine!" said Boyo. "Do you feel able to give an independent opinion?"

"Certainly," I said. He looked amazed, relieved, and a bit shaken. "Now, will anyone else be giving evidence?"

"There are supposed to be two others—I don't know whom he's got, but Fundament will tell you."

"I can see Fundament about it, can I? It might be wise."

"Yes, splendid idea—I'll see if I can get him. Can you go round now if he's free?"

I told him I'd be delighted, and I was looking forward to meeting him. Boyo gave me a quick look as if he suspected I was being ironical about something, but decided I wasn't. I must have looked too innocent, or too serious. Boyo was not really clever. He was suddenly wreathed in smiles.

"That's a relief," he said. "You know, Georgie, I don't mind telling you I thought you were going to be difficult, or have scruples, or something—you're so damned suspicious."

"That sort of attitude," I said, "must make life very difficult for people like you."

"Precisely." He buzzed for a line, gave his number, and asked for the Foreign Secretary. The relish with which he asked was terrible to me—it wasn't just the relish with which he'd ask for one steak, but as if he were asking for all the steaks he'd ever have. In fact, no doubt, he was.

"Thank you, thank you, splendid." Click. "Fundament'll see you in twenty minutes. I'll send a car. Now, about premises. Since you'll be here some time—don't hesitate to ask me. I know all the ropes."

I gathered my possessions. Boyo's No. 1 chauffeur appeared in the corridor. "If you don't want to live alone," said

Boyo, "there are some very nice youngsters on my staff—I pick them—introduce you later. Bye!"

"Boys or girls?" I hissed, but he'd gone.

I didn't actually spit on Boyo's carpet. I was saving my ammunition for Fundament, and I was dead glad to be seeing him while the effects of that blackguard report were still warm on me. The floor had stopped sinking. Now I'd read the thing, I would be a street musician, or even a street sweeper, with a song in my heart, for just as long as necessary to cover the pleasure of the "independent opinion" I was going to give Fundament, and the sight of his face when I'd given it.

Boyo's office was the most modern type of humbug factory. Fossil-Fundament's was traditional: the plant was different, that is, though the product was the same. Where Boyo's waiting room had glass and sansevierias in pots, Fundament's had mahogany and British Council publications. Boyo had two originals, Dufy and Bernard Buffet—Fundament had a set of royal portraits (ace, joker, queen, and two knaves, which was a first-rate poker hand, if he hadn't let everybody see it)—and a nonroyal portrait of a salmon with the middle cut removed in a very heavy gold frame. Probably this had a safe behind it, and it was the cheapest canvas they could get which was big enough. The oddest decoration in Fundament's anteroom was a full-size tailor's dummy, standing in front of a pier glass like a suit of armor; it wore a 1930 lounge suit and shiny shoes. The chairs were actually more comfortable than Boyo's—plush, like Mother's lap, but hard to get out of quickly; so that Fundament could be sure of having you a little ruffled when he summoned you in. The whole place was purposely solid, purposely, that is, in the sense of blindly cunning intuition which is the Fundament substitute for purpose, earthquakeproof, not only unchanged but meant to show you that it was unchangeable, with a touch of the library and the Head's study to strike a note of intimidation. It was finely and intuitively adjusted to flatten out Englishmen—I wondered if Fundament was smart enough to have a different one for foreigners; for example, the note of railway station and Madame would have spoiled it completely for a Frenchman. What I couldn't understand was the dummy. It didn't seem to be part of the scheme, and I couldn't follow the intuition behind it, unless it was meant to make you feel you were watched, or as a trap to make you rehearse your piece out loud with it so that Fundament could take you off-center and looking silly.

It wasn't for ten minutes that I discovered what it was for. I hadn't been watching it closely, because there wasn't any doubt what it was, only why Fundament had it there. I'd started a jolly British Council publication about hunting with the Quorn when the dummy said: "Well, I'm afraid the Minister's still engaged. But I don't think he'll keep you long. I think I'd better go and see. Excuse me."

And it opened the door into the inner office and peered round it with the precaution of an Indian stalking bison. It took a full minute after the door closed in letting go the handle, to make sure the thing didn't make a noise.

Then it said, "I think he'll be ready in a moment. I think we're actually a little early."

So the dummy was the cleverest dodge of the lot. The intuitive confidence men had still got the edge on the calculating, Boyo variety. Boyo would never have thought of dressing his secretary as a dummy. He was more likely to choose one he could undress. Years of English upper-class experience without one thought in its head was still intuitively cleverer at its job than Boyo, who went at the game scientifically but didn't believe in it. By contrast the Establishment had actually succeeded in kidding itself. The dummy had even me rattled.

"Haven't we met before?" I asked it.

"Possibly—have you called on the Minister before?"

"No," I said, "but I've seen you. I'm sure of it."

"Yes? Any particular place?"

"In Horne Bros. window. I know I have."

"Yes? I doubt it, you know—I don't actually *go* there; usually Austin Reed's—still, medical men have a memory for faces, I know. But I don't remember being in there lately."

Not a twitch. He was solid tortoiseshell, guaranteed. There was a silly little buzzer like a perfect gentleman trying to shout quietly.

"The Minister will see you now," said Horne Bros. "This way."

Horne Bros. was the first part of the shock treatment. As I went through the door of the inner office I got the second part.

The enormous desk and the rest of the décor I'd expected. What I hadn't expected was Fossil-Fundament himself. He wasn't real either. If Boyo was glossy and Horne Bros. was stuffed, he was waxy. His bright blue eye, a great electoral asset, I'd been told, could hardly be artificial, but all the rest might have been, and a surprising amount of it obviously was. The bronzed glow of health hadn't gone quite far enough down to the collar when he put it on. His lips were not only bright red but shiny like nail polish. He had an elaborate, curly coiffure which didn't at first sight appear to be made of human hair. He smelt faintly of resin. God, I thought, he's been embalmed. He was coming at me with "Ah, come in, sit down" and a manic extended hand, but even this was a rehearsed gesture—I was too astonished by the close sight of him to react immediately, and he had to stop at the prearranged mark on the carpet, his arm sagging like a stuck trafficator, until I got there to shake it.

I only recovered when we were settled, and then I realized that somehow he was enormously gratified. Evidently he'd taken my reaction for awe at the Presence.

"We were all very grateful to you, Doctor, for your promptness in coming back to Europe. I'm only sorry we couldn't explain the reason we wanted you. But I'll do that now—I'm sure you want to know." The varnished crack extended itself from ear to ear, and then regained its normal dimensions. Obviously, I'd come back to Europe by the next boat simply to do his bidding, and I was going to be overjoyed to hear my orders.

"We want a confirmatory opinion." Long pause, in which I was expected to ask for details. I said nothing.

"We want a confirmatory opinion on a question which comes, I think, within your field. It's a matter of some diplomatic importance to the—Friworld—" (the expression came out as a single word, with a dropped voice, and much the throwaway intonation which a BBC announcer would use if he had to report a case of bestiality). "We are being rather seriously misrepresented in the United Nations about our recent weapon trials. No doubt you've read the papers. The story, of course, is that we are adversely affecting the fertility of the Asian countries; it's an ideal story, you'll agree, from the psychological warfare point of view. We want to rebut it. It seems virtually certain that the Assembly will insist on an inquiry. Now there are two matters in which you can help us. We shall of course be producing our own experts, but we want the opinion of an independent, responsible scientist who has lived in Asia and carries weight there."

"I see."

He tried to look through this and couldn't. "Now I've no doubt, of course, that you'll support the general line our men will take. It's possible that we shall have to agree to actual experiments under international supervision. Now in that case we would wish that the independent expert who conducted them should be conversant with our side of the case. If your testimony were satisfactory—*if* it were satisfactory—the Cabinet has authorized me to offer you the responsibility for conducting those tests." The blue eyes twinkled as they were switched on, and the varnished crack snapped into a jolly smile.

"Might I know," I said, "who your own experts will be?"

"Well, we shall be hearing evidence from Dr. Cannon." He paused to let Cannon sink in. Chief bomb maker, I thought, clever overgrown schoolboy, vast technical-school inferiority complex, hell-bent on a knighthood, who can be flattered into anything in consequence. Stooge number one.

"Cannon's not a biologist, of course."

"No," said Fundament, "he will be dealing with the physical aspect, naturally. The medical side will be represented by Sir Frank Pus."

Ten years ago, before he became a whole-time adviser on matters he doesn't understand, he was a very successful society gynecologist, as long as he didn't actually operate. I knew, because I used to be his R.S.O. Presumably he's in this via the word fertility. Stooge number two.

"And biology?" I asked.

"We were hoping to rely on you."

"I see," I said. "In other words, you want someone with some knowledge of the subject to endorse what these two have agreed to say." And I gave him his own jolly smile straight back.

For a moment the penny didn't drop. Then the salesmanship rolled off his face from below upward, like a window shade, and disappeared into his coiffure.

"We naturally wanted an honest opinion—an honest and responsible opinion from you."

"Knowing that neither of your experts knows the first thing about the subject, and that the evidence they're going to give will be untrue?" I asked him.

"I resent that suggestion. We naturally expect a man of science to approach a public issue like this without a preconceived basis. You haven't read their evidence. How do you know it won't be true?"

"I have read the literature, which is more than they've done," I said, "and I know that if they were going to speak the truth you wouldn't have invited them to testify."

"I resent that very much indeed."

"Good," I said. "And I resent being brought away from work of real importance to support a political swindle disguised as science. I know the facts in this matter, and so do you—they've been reported to you often enough by experts you won't be calling."

"Really? The facts are capable of conflicting interpretations."

"So is the date on the calendar. Either of your men would gladly say that Wednesday was Friday after a few gins and a royal handshake or two."

"Dr. Goggins!" said Fundament, displaying more self-control than I'd expected, though his makeup was beginning to run. "I wish you'd credit other people beside yourself with some sincerity of intention. I find your position illogical, I must say. You spend your life working to reduce fertility in Asia, and yet you're outraged if the requirements of defense are suspected—merely suspected, I repeat—of producing a very small, barely measurable effect of the same kind. In spite of what you've just said Dr. Cannon and Sir Frank have produced a most imposing case in our favor."

"That naturally depends whom it's supposed to impose upon," I said. "You'd better borrow Dr. Untergang from the Americans—he'll not only testify for you, he'll produce fake experimental data as necessary."

He began to swell up like a bird getting ready to wash.

"Incidentally," I went on, "I *have* read your document—I conclude that Untergang wrote most of it, and as it's chiefly science fiction that seems highly probable."

"May I ask where you saw this supposed document?"

"Boyo showed it to me."

"Who??"

"I'm sorry—Jebb Jollyboy, O.B.E."

"He had no right," said Fundament, "to do anything of the kind. It is a highly confidential document."

"That I don't doubt," I said. "But I didn't want you to be able to say that I made up my mind without seeing the story I was supposed to swear to. I'll bet the other two haven't seen it. In any case there's nothing whatever secret about that essay of Untergang's. Everyone knows what your experts will say, and everyone knows that if they weren't going to say it, you wouldn't consult them."

"Well, if that's how you feel, Dr. Goggins," said Fundament, "there's no more to be said. But I must say I'm disappointed. You'll allow me to point out that we have consulted a supposedly independent expert—yourself—and you've refused to testify."

"Who's refused to testify?"

"You have. Clearly in view of the sentiments you've been expressing I must take your remarks as a refusal—of a rather gratuitously offensive kind, if I may say so."

"On the contrary," I said, "I insist upon testifying. I'm going to do exactly what you've asked me to do—give an independent biological opinion. Are we all agreed?"

"I shall decide," said Fundament, "to whom we entrust the presentation of the—er—Friworld's—case. And it won't be you. After this interview I'm not surprised to learn that you came to Paris in the first instance at the request of the Russians." I didn't rise to this, because I'd heard the click as the tape recorder went on, and in any case he telegraphed it like a novice. "We shall entrust it," he went on, when it was quite clear I hadn't bitten, "to people who know how our confidence should be treated."

"I know," I said, "how your confidence should be treated," and for the benefit of the tape I told him in precise but easily understood anatomical terms exactly what I thought he ought to do with it.

He turned his back ostentatiously at the first Anglo-Saxon word and rang for Horne Bros. The moment the door opened, down rolled his bargain-sale expression from among his front curls and pulled itself over his chin.

"Dr. Goggins," he said, blue-eyeing handsomely. Out went the trafficator hand. I walked straight through it.

Horne Bros. trotted along behind.

"I trust that was satisfactory?" he said.

"Very satisfactory."

"Good." My God, I thought, he's hovering. *Num tu, Brute?* It can't be—those buttons surely aren't practicable.

"Dr. Goggins, forgive me, but are you in a hurry?"

So they were practicable, after all. "Not particularly," I said.

"I don't like to delay you, but I was wondering if you could possibly help me over a personal matter."

His collar was stretched to the limit. He was finding this as arduous as reproduction is to the tortoise.

"You are an expert on fertility?"

"On human mating behavior generally."

"Would that include. . . ?"

I told him it would and suggested we have a drink over it.

Horne Bros.' problem was a pretty simple one. I told him what to do, and said that if he hadn't got results in a fortnight I'd talk to his wife as well. He was exhausted but happy. The catharsis had almost melted him—he must have gone straight to change his linen.

With all this, I'd kept Dulcinea waiting: she was never late. From the bottom of the Samaritaine escalator I could see her among the colored-print fabrics. The escalators are slippery —one is not expected to help them by running. On the way up I passed an exhibit extending three floors which was of real use to me from the semantic point of view—it classified teen-age brassieres under the headings "bientôt," "déjà," "enfin." Add "assez, assez," and this terminology was exactly what I needed for my somatotypology work. Unfortunately I didn't maintain the example of tact it gave me.

"Did you see the man?" said Dulcinea when we'd kissed, she picking up one heel to do it like a Thoroughbred jumper, which is one of her nicest gestures.

"I saw him."

"You're grinning horribly. I ought to have come with you—you've said something dreadful to him."

"I don't think I overdid it."

"Tell me what you said!"

"I said, Miss Fuentes and McGredy, I love you—to think that one inch more and the Pope would have got you!"

"I'm not being kissed," said Dulcinea, "until you tell me what you said to him."

"Not here, because there's a notice over there 'English

spoken,' and I'm tired of you telling me I'm coarse when I'm really only blunt and forthright."

"Well, what did he want you to do?"

"He wanted," I said, "to make me play the Dad to all the gallimaufry that is stuffed in his corrupted, bastard-bearing womb."

"*What?*"

"Say, strumpet, must I?"

"Don't call me strumpet, I don't like it. And talk sense."

"Quotation," I said, "from *'Tis Pity She's a Whore.*"

I might have learned tact from the notices.

"Are you trying to hurt my feelings?" said Dulcinea. "I'm not a whore."

I could have kicked myself for trying to be funny. One day I'd learn to keep my mouth shut. But nothing seemed to get Dulcinea down for long—in minutes she was perky again. We passed the furs on the way out, and I stopped and held her round the waist, high up.

"What will you like for your birthday?" I asked her, giving her a fair chance at the furs.

"Is it tomorrow, or something?"

"No, the day after. The twenty-second."

"I'd forgotten." No sign of surprise that I knew: it was the first time that my precaution of getting the birthday date at the outset hadn't paid off. "You still haven't told me what you'd like," I said.

"Anything nice and not expensive"—not looking at the furs, but at a little invisible inscription floating just over my head—"except information!"

Evidently she wasn't going to be a woman who lived by bread alone.

There were two other urgent calls I had to make. One was at the Institute of Human Biology—there at least, since I and not Boyo had arranged it, there were no serious snags. I had a good room, the facilities I wanted for the fertility project were ready, and they'd even ordered the glassware.

The only trouble was that my next-door neighbor, who was a perfume chemist, appeared to be making poison gas, because he'd fitted two high-delivery blowers to ventilate his stink cupboard, and these shook the whole floor. I made up my mind to check whether they were shaking the balance room as well, before having my balance set up, but that would do later.

The other call I was pretty sure wouldn't succeed—that was to call on Tarunachandra, who was Indian scientific attaché and an old classmate of mine who'd taken the psychiatric half of my earlier fertility work in India. I was wanting to see if he'd been able to shorten my sabbatical leave, but I knew it wasn't very likely that he could do anything now. He hadn't held out much hope before I left on the tour, and he was as good as his word: the locum tenens was in, and they couldn't sack him to reinstate me.

"This is a pity," he said, "but at least we'll have your company. You will have no difficulty, working."

I told him I wasn't so sure—Chandra had a clinic of his own two afternoons a week. As the only Indian-born psychoanalyst I've met who has practiced both at home and in Europe, I think he had a resistance to the idea of letting me go home early, in view of a plan we had made to meet regularly and talk about the cross-cultural experience he was getting, which would take quite two years. I asked him if he could get me a clinic job, in the fertility side. Possibly we could work together on the factors in anxiety which alter fertility. Even this bait didn't draw a salary, however, though I knew he'd do his best.

I also told him about Dulcinea; the interesting thing to both of us, behaviorally, was the speed of the pickup, and the way in which it had arranged itself. I'd never experienced this before: so far as I could judge, looking inward, in the very first instance a sudden hostility to Otto was what set it off—I'd barely felt the jolt, but the inner man had virtually rescued the mother-heroine and committed me up to the ears before I realized she was even attractive. Perhaps without Otto she wouldn't have been. "It makes me wonder," I told Chandra, "whether we weren't up the wrong tree when we were working on mate selection; we ought to have looked into all the cases where somebody's effectively rescued a daughter from his own bad father figure."

"Not many of our series, if I remember, have so quickly pinched older men's wives," said Chandra, with a very straight face. "Anyhow, does the superego approve the performance? Was she worth it by daylight?"

I said it was too soon to say, but I was pretty sure she was well worth it, and I ought to stand my unconscious a drink for collecting her; anyhow, Chandra would be meeting her if we were going to write up his cases together. I also told him about Fundament. He asked if I'd noticed any resemblance to Otto.

"Why?"

"Because that makes two fathers who have bitten the dust at your hands lately; the inner man seems to be having a field day; you would be wise to notice the tendency, or more will be coming later. However," he said, "I have seen Fundament, and here too the event is highly satisfactory to me. I'd like to have said all those rude things myself. But you know, George, on duty we'd wonder what was wrong with that man, why he is governing the world out of his nursery like the rest of them. Most satisfying to tell him to go to hell, but it is our pretention to cure him for the general good. This he will never have, but is it possible? That would be here the question. Not that I'd like to try."

"If I hadn't been so bloody rude he might pay me to cure him," I said, "but it isn't my speciality. At least I'd hate to see him fertile—think of the place swimming with Fundaments at the tadpole stage."

"I doubt if we run any risk," said Chandra. "I doubt the strength of his heterosexuality would run to it, if you did. Now you must go and look for a job. You can count on me."

However, theory apart, I was no nearer an income, with an unexpected female dependent to support—in comfort if possible: I owed it to her. And Dr. Otto had had a very expensive camera.

Dulcinea, sitting up in bed at the hotel in Robinson, where I'd settled her, poured out our breakfast coffee and listened gravely to my financial and other difficulties. To keep out the crumbs she'd pulled the sheet up level with her two little breasts—the kind that are still "déja" rather than "enfin," though she isn't as young as that: I'd already christened the left one Jean-Jacques Rousseau. That morning I noticed they had quarreled, as the Italians say, and turned their backs on each other, and I remember thinking I must make a note when they did it next, as it was probably cyclical and certainly charming.

I explained, meanwhile, that I'd just got to find some way of keeping us while I got on with my work at the institute. I'd got everything there except a personal income.

"At any rate," she said, "don't worry. I'll have to get a job—I'll be bored otherwise. We'll manage."

All night something had been fitting itself together in my head—it included Dulcinea, and some Americans we'd seen at the Casino de Paris, who'd brought field glasses—not opera glasses, mind you, but things the size of astronomical telescopes —Chandra's remarks, and my own work, and Horne Bros. with his marital problems. It was just on the point of falling into place.

I told Dulcinea I was on the verge of an idea that just didn't come, but I knew the technique for catching it. If I made love to her at once it would click in the few minutes' relaxation afterwards.

"Not with the tray here," she said, firmly. "I'm going to finish my coffee."

In fact, it fell together while she was drinking the last cup.

"Look," I said, "why don't we teach?"

"What, languages? I've tried that. There are hundreds of White Russians doing that. And you don't want to coach students—it would be a waste of your qualifications."

"I didn't mean that. Why can't we teach the one thing we really do know about?"

"What's that?"

"What we've just been doing."

She looked up and wondered, quite serious, reading the little inscription just over my head. "But don't they know that already?"

"Well, how many men have you met who knew it already?"

"None. Not even you—you may be a professional expert, but I think I'm teaching you something."

"So there's something to teach, and we can teach it."

"By correspondence? Or I suppose it could be part of your human biology course. We might even get on television. Silly!"

"I'm perfectly serious," I said, "and I don't even exclude television, eventually."

She looked down from the overhead inscription. "I believe you are—" she said, and looked at me for a change.

"Why shouldn't I be? It's both our professions."

Dulcinea sat bolt upright, pulled up the lace on the sheet like barbed wire, and started to put Jean-Jacques and the other chap away.

"I don't think that's nice, even if you're being funny. If you aren't being funny, you wouldn't like it when it came to the point—anyhow they'd deport you for living on my earnings. Even Otto never tried that one on me."

I explained that I didn't mean that, and she ought to have known it. What I had in mind was something perfectly ethical and far more revolutionary.

"We'd hold classes."

"Idiot!"

"Look," I said, "this is the one subject in which every émigré Englishman and American is interested. They have virtually no other reason for living. Yet it's the one subject about which they can't get really practical information. They try to get it from sex books, which never teach any figures beyond the quarter turns. They try to get it from pornography —and either get swindled or read a lot of pathological bunk. They try to get it from whores, then resent their wives for not cooperating. If they had what we have, it would radically alter their experience of life."

"Tell me when to applaud the speech," said Dulcinea. "You were just going to make me hold classes."

"Classes for married couples only, directed by a registered medical practitioner, smelling strongly of carbolic—no Paul Joneses allowed; demonstrations with models—all blameless; exercises—in thick drawers; we start with a preliminary series of briefing lectures and group problem discussions, then the sexes separate and we each take half the class. Then, if it takes on, we do a book—class members only—all the difficult bits from Chinese, Sanskrit, or Arabic so that they're classical. If the organ starts to play, we're helping to safeguard Christian matrimony by improving relations within marriage: if it plays very loud, we have special classes for Catholics with a cleric in charge and a kosher syllabus. Full psychiatric and medical supervision, no big fees, no secrecy, all sweetness and light. And they'd get value—my God, they'd get value."

Dulcinea stared at my enthusiasm for a full thirty seconds; finally she said, "I really believe you *are* serious. I'll have to assume you are."

"It's a serious business."

"And I know you haven't been drinking—only coffee." She began to think visibly. "We could never get away with it," she said, at last.

"You forget I've got the front door key. I'm a registered medical practitioner and an international expert on human mating behavior. I've published papers and addressed conferences about it. Governments consult me. So does everyone else who can do it on the quiet and gratis. All I want to do is to convert my assets into a remunerated service to humanity: fair?"

"All that would happen," said Dulcinea, firmly, "is that they'd strike you off the register—for advertising, if nothing else—and you'd have to be a quack, like Otto."

"But we wouldn't advertise," I said. "They come and pester me already: it would go round by word of mouth. Anyhow, if we played our cards right we'd have it given out from the pulpit of the Anglo-American church here, free, gratis and for nothing."

"What about the General Medical Council?"

I explained to her. Nothing, bar crime, is unethical in medicine unless your colleagues resent it. They resent it if you cut them out: we would cut them in. They react if you use the wrong names for things and shock them: we would use the right names. Abortion is unethical—therapeutic termination of pregnancy isn't. Sticking one's neck out is unethical—"so," I said, "we won't stick it out. We'll move forward behind a solid screen of consultants and churchmen. You speak English perfectly. But you don't understand the use that can be made of the English language. This whole thing depends on saying things in the right way. People are struck off for barging ahead saying the wrong thing. If whores would only call themselves substitutional therapists and work through the proper channels they could have a Royal College, with professional examinations, before you could say Nell Gwyn. In England you can talk your way into anything and out of anything if you give things the right names."

"You can talk yourself into Dartmoor," said Dulcinea, "but not out—or perhaps you can. Who do you think our pupils will be?"

I explained the rest of my idea. Initially, we would concentrate on the Free World. Paris, as I had seen, was full of these unhappy, overanxious, overpaid, oversexed Anglo-Americans, middle-class people who staffed the various stooge-military and sham-cultural organizations. Most of them had frustrated, unoccupied wives, nothing significant to do, and no recreations but adultery and nuclear weapons. There was no intention of exploiting them—we would make no attempt to compete with the teachers of yoga, Moral Rearmament, relaxation, or right thinking, and we wouldn't expound a philosophy. We would give these people, if they were able to take it, their first real experience of pleasure, and see if it helped them or civilized them at all. I expected that quite half the benefit would come, not from any techniques we could teach them, but simply from the sense of permission implied in being taught. We would have to arrange the course to weed out those who'd be disturbed by it (we'd have a stress session so that they could be disturbed in the first lecture and leave). By the end of a week of talking it would be obvious who could benefit and who would be better left alone. These expatriates, particularly middle-class English and admin-class Americans, would be quite the best material—living in France always makes them wish they were adults (the French would find the whole thing really funny, but it wasn't going to be directed at them).

Dulcinea was still thinking—but not about what I was saying.

"Will we go to England?" she asked, when I'd finished.

I knew what was really in her mind, marriage, and Otto, and her own security. I explained we had to keep this out of England at first. The Free Worlders were an offbeat community where I knew it could take root. After that we'd see. But I didn't see why we shouldn't eventually take it to England. We would need to do it either via the Church or via the Establishment. Possibly we could produce a soap-and-incense flavored brand for the Marriage Guidance Council. Possibly we could hook Royalty in some way. We'd wait and see what came.

"I can see the Church and Royalty supporting this kind of thing," said Dulcinea. "I can see them putting up with me."

"You forget," I told her, "our bishops marry."

"But not for fun."

"You haven't got it—we don't attempt to sell them fun. You never mention fun in England. That isn't the line at all. We are concerned to make the Christian, one-shot theory of monogamy work. God insists that you buy your meat in unopened cans, one each, no inspection of contents, no guarantee, and if the contents are off you eat them and like them or go without: that's what morality is about. Well and good. We show them how to make curry. We are the saviors of marriage."

"When we aren't married ourselves."

I told her I was sure that in the end we would be able to put that right if we still wanted, or if we had to for business reasons. Till then we were professional partners.

She was still sad about this. I knew why she wanted to go to England. "It isn't the whole of marriage," she said.

"No, but it will give them something to do. After all, it gives us something to do. And if I say it's the perfect release of tension you'll savage me, but it is."

She put the tray over the side of the bed and got well into my arms. "I love you," she said, "even if you're quite mad. You may be what you call bloody-minded, but at least you aren't a swine." That was one of the nicest compliments I ever received. It was the first time either of us had used the word love in the regular sense, and I noticed that from Dulcinea it no longer worried me. Obviously we were going to be together for a long time—even if the classes didn't materialize. I told her that I loved her too, and I meant it in every sense.

At that point the phone by the bedside rang. The voice was Boyo's.

"Hullo, Goggins, is that you?"

I had the wind in my tail from Dulcinea and my new scheme, and I felt too good to be bothered with Boyo. I answered no, that I was at present living in Pakistan under the assumed name of John Thomas, and this was my little brother speaking, but I'd give myself a message. Dulcinea kicked me. "That's what I mean," she said.

"I've seen Fundament," I told him.

"Yes, don't I know it? The whole place is ringing with it. And look here—you betrayed my confidence: I showed you that thing strictly on the q.t. He's been on the phone here after my blood. And yours—I was going to warn you to look out."

"I never enjoyed an interview more," I said. "It was well worth it. Thank you for arranging the trip."

"Well, you needn't blame me," said Boyo. "I wasn't to know."

"If Fundament was in it you could bet it was crooked, and I might have guessed it."

"Of course I knew it was going to be crooked," he said, "but I didn't know it was going to be the sort of crooked you'd object to. Here, have you got a bird there listening?"

I kept my temper and only told him that Fundament had probably had his phone tapped and he would be listening.

Boyo subsided and asked me if I'd got a job, and if there was anything he could do. I told him I'd got not a job, but an idea, and he could let me know if Sir Frank Pus lived in France still, and where.

"Well, insofar as he's alive at all, he lives at the Hôtel des Alpes Maritimes at Cannes," said Boyo. "Don't tell me he's the other expert. Look, you have got a bird there with you, because I can hear her."

"I'm sorry," I said, "I can't discuss state secrets. But thanks."

"Look out for Fundament," said Boyo and rang off.

"What was all that?" asked Dulcinea.

"Just a friendly warning that they're after my blood. Would you like a weekend at Cannes?"

"I'd love it," she said, then "Can we afford it?" then "No, I'd rather not." I could see the worries going across her face like patches of low cloud.

"Why not?"

"We might meet Otto."

"Did he say he was going there?" I asked her.

"No, but he will. It's full of rich old ladies with pains in their necks."

"Then never mind him. You leave him to me. Get up, and we'll go round and book on the Mistral. I've still got some of Fundament's travel expenses left."

She still wasn't happy, and to tell the truth neither was I. Even if there wasn't the off chance of running into Otto we needed to be careful. I'd been stunningly indiscreet. Fundament would have put the smear machine into full gear, I knew, to make sure I didn't get myself a hearing privately at the conference or leak anything to the press. It only needed Otto to catch up with us and make trouble to do me a lot of harm. He wouldn't play up his marital rights, I was pretty sure, but he might accuse Dulcinea of stealing, for example, and I, like an ass, hadn't even checked what she brought away. If she had picked me up, instead of I her, I'd even have wondered if both she and Otto were part of Fundament's precautions in case I was uncooperative, but it seemed quite unlikely. Then I wondered if the pair of them really had picked me up, and done it rather well, but that didn't seem likely either. However, I resolved to face a very unpleasant duty. As soon as I got a chance I dropped a note to Chandra, who had diplomatic facilities, to say Dulcinea was *his* mistress and check her with the Paris Fraud Squad and Interpol—not that I cared what her record was, so long as it didn't include blackmail, but I couldn't risk leaving any shot in Fundament's locker that I didn't know about. For good measure I included Otto. She was clear. I heard that night. So was he.

All the way to Cannes I felt like Tolstoi on his wedding night, because I loved her and don't like humbug. Finally, when she began worrying about Otto again, as we got near Arles, I gave her a deliberate hint. "Otto can't touch us so far as I know," I told her, "and you've got no police record."

Dulcinea was doing crochet without watching her fingers, which always baffles me.

"Did you look me up?" she said, placid as ever, reading the little inscription over my head.

"Yes. I'm sorry, but I did."

"Well, of course—it was only sensible," she said. "I thought you would. And I went and checked you with the Sûreté. I wanted to make quite sure you were real."

I felt I had never admired women more, which is saying a great deal.

When I'd last seen Sir Frank he had been larger than life too—better turned out than Horne Bros., livelier than Boyo,

much more plausible than Fundament, and genial to a turn.
By contrast, he was real enough, though hardly genuine. He
was the Great Surgeon—when he put his fingertips together
you could almost see the hundreds of society pelvises they had
explored. Some of their aristocracy had rubbed off on him. He
was not only comely, an unaging pushover like a masculine and
virile Cleopatra—he had class, which none of the Boyos or the
Fundaments could touch. He had learned long since not to
operate on anything difficult in case it died: the society preg-
nancies he had terminated would have stretched, foetus to
foetus, round Trafalgar Square—there was one of his little silver
wire rings inside every expensive "hostess" in Europe, and the
trade routes had carried them all over the world. As against
that, he always had the decency to help as many poor-girls-in-
trouble out of trouble, without charge, as the Director of Public
Prosecutions would swear. With that distinguished white head
and sonorous voice in the dock, the D.P.P. would never have
had a chance, the jury would have carried him out shoulder
high, and the judge would have made a note of his address
for future family reference. He wasn't an ethical ornament to
the profession, but he wasn't vicious; in fact, he was basically
kindly. The pomposity was part of his patter, not a built-in
self-deception like Fundament's. Somebody else, I thought,
who filled Dulcinea's definition of me—only he'd never run
the risk of being bloody-minded.

It was a shock, when the waiter pointed him out, to see how
he'd shrunk. He was no longer big—he hardly filled the wicker
chair he was sitting in, he had a white, senescent hat that
seemed to be pressing him down, and his face and hands had
gone an infant pink. God, I think, is evidently just; Sir Frank
is turning into a foetus again, until death winkles him out of
his womb in Cannes, and that operation will certainly be free.

I stood in front of him, by the glass of milk on the table,
until he came out of *The Times*.

"Do you want me?" he said. "Now—if it wasn't for the
moustache I'd say George Goggins, and by your color you've
been out East somewhere. Right?"

His voice had run up, too, like a plant under a barrel, and it was thin now instead of rolling. When he'd had an attractive patient in hand it used to be like Old Man River. But at least he'd spotted me and remembered me.

"What are you doing here? Not come to see me?"

"Well, yes and no," I said, "I was in Cannes, and I've just heard you were, so I've come over to buy you a drink."

"It'll have to be milk," he said. "Never mind—it's about the most expensive drink here; comes by air, you know—there are no cows in the South of France. Sit down!"

I asked him if he was seeing patients.

"Only myself—if I were a woman I'd be expected to cure myself; as it is, I know I can't. Do you know any cure for old age?"

"You used to prescribe Woman," I reminded him, "you used to quote Rabelais—only women are rejuvenated by the magic fountain, but the way to rejuvenate a man is through commerce with one of them who's had the treatment."

"Don't throw that up at me, my boy—I've left it too long."

"You're retired, are you, now, sir?"

"No, oh no, I'm the other thing. I'm an expert. They send me stuff to read and I tell 'em if it's all right. I don't have to stand, for that—I can do it chairborne. So I'm still cheating the devil. If I retired I'd be gone in a month—you ought to know that."

"That's textbooks, and refereeing, I suppose?" I said, as innocently as I could manage.

"Good God, no! I'm a government expert. The whole of our national effort turns on me, though you won't believe it— I sit here and tell them when they're writing nonsense about fertility and childbirth and so on: with all this radiation they've suddenly realized that fertility matters, entertainment apart. I've been trying to make them see that for thirty years, so now I tell them what to say."

This was according to plan, so I started to close in.

"You aren't on this United Nations thing, are you, sir?"

"I didn't think that was public," he said. "Are you on it now? You should be—it's far more your line than mine."

"Well," I said, "they wanted me to be, in confidence, but I didn't feel very happy about the case they were making."

"You've seen this report thing, have you? I haven't seen it—what's it like? Is it a good job of work?" As I thought—no doubt Cannon hadn't seen it either.

"Frankly, I think it's very doubtful," I said. "There's a lot of bad experimental work in it."

He picked up the milk and drank it halfway.

"Well, of course," he said, "you're a scientist. But we've got to be practical. We all know they've got to put up a case. You know what's behind it, I expect. It's all bombs. This Communist talk about infertility in Africa—it's a dodge to stop us testing them—so apparently it's quite important. To the nation and the government and all that. I told myself, after all, they're batting for the home side: we ought to pull our weight, you know."

The question was, how to make him uneasy about it. Ethics were out, so first I tried science: I told him some of the things which were in the report—including all the stuff of Untergang's which nobody else had been able to repeat. He didn't look worried about the discrepancies.

"You got these data from Fossil-Fundament?"

"Not directly, but they came from him."

"You don't imagine Her Majesty's ministers would get facts like that wrong, do you?" said Sir Frank. "They're responsible chaps. You know, you've been out of Europe, Goggins—all those other experiments were probably done by a lot of Communists. I'd take the home side's word for it, I think—they're usually not far wrong. And in a war, you know, you have to stretch things a bit sometimes—I remember in Messpot . . ."

While he was retelling that, my mind jogged my elbow and gave me a note. On it was a name.

"Well, I'll reconsider it," I said, "you've set my mind at rest about the report. I'll be quite frank with you, though—the real reason I wasn't happy about the facts being right was this business of Pybus being mixed up with it. But if *you're* satisfied, I certainly am."

Sir Frank jumped violently and choked.

"Pybus mixed up with it? What's he been up to?"

I thought: afterwards I must buy my preconscious mind a drink.

Sir Frank had been on his last mouthful of milk after the Messpot story, but he seemed to have found a depth charge in it. This wasn't surprising. Pybus was the gynecologist who'd beaten Sir Frank to the Queen of Silesia's fibroid, and removed it—when Sir Frank had diagnosed it as a baby prince. They'd bought a royal layette. The saying had always been that Sir Frank had had a finger in every pie and commonly pulled out a plum, but the Queen of Silesia's fibroid wasn't one of them—and since this little contretemps Pybus wasn't normally mentioned by name in Sir Frank's firm. I'd had his name handed me on a slip by the same level of my mind that had negotiated with Dulcinea and handed *her* to me—again, just at the right moment.

"Only," I said, taking its advice implicitly and letting it improvise from then on—"that I rather *think* you may have been consulted at Pybus's suggestion."

"You do, do you?"

"Yes, I rather *think* you may have been. I thought you ought to know."

"Well, I'll be . . ." Sir Frank had learned long ago to leave the most harmless swearing unvoiced. It avoided accidents with Royalty. But I knew quite a few words he was thinking.

"I thought as a matter of fact you probably did know about it," I said; "I thought probably you didn't like to rock the home side's boat."

"I most certainly did *not* know about it—but I see a lot of things now. By George! I'll rock Pybus's boat for him—if he recommended them to ask me, he must *know* the thing's a disgrace. He won't touch it, so he hopes I will."

"Surely not," I said, "and he'd know in any case that you'd criticize the experiments."

"He knows as well as you do that I don't know a blessed thing about them—I'm taking the Ministry's word, backing them up and all that—evidently he hopes I'm caught out over it. What a trick!"

I deprecated this again, decrescendo.

"You came down to tip me off, now, didn't you?"

"Well, as a matter of fact, yes."

"And you didn't like to give away a confidence, so you waited until I'd told you I was in the know. I very much appreciate it. You've saved me from making a very big mistake."

"You won't withdraw, will you?" I said.

"Well, not exactly that—one doesn't 'withdraw.' But I'm old enough to be damned ill." Once he'd have said "dashed," when he was in practice, probably not that. He was most careless with that, as he was with his collars now. But so far from being hurt by having to drop the expert business he looked younger angry, younger by quite a year since I mentioned Pybus. I'd got him well in motion.

"I'm most deeply obliged to you, Goggins. Coming down here specially."

"No, I wanted some sea air in any case," I said. "I'll be working for two years in Paris, I hope. I'll be down again if I can afford it."

"If there's ever anything I can do for you, don't hesitate to ask," said Sir Frank.

"Well, as a matter of fact, there is," I said, and I told him in outline about the fun and games clinic, in terms he'd be likely to approve. In fact I told him most of the scheme, but with the medical pedal hard down. The key of the exposition must have been right.

"I think it's a capital idea, if you don't have trouble with the Church, my boy. If I was younger I'd come and teach myself—I'm much too old to be got in the family way now."

"It was because of the Church I thought possibly you might be able to help me get started," I told him. "If you could see your way to give us some support, I want to build up a really eminent medical panel of sponsors to prove that the thing is honest and kosher—bishops too, if they'll come in. I can give you my word that you won't be let in for anything troublesome."

"I'll be delighted to give you any support in my power. I quite agree. It's time we put this thing on a proper, sensible basis. I only wish *I'd* known more when I married."

He wrote me a letter.

"One last thing," the old boy said, as I thanked him. "I know what you think about me. You think I'm a silly old so-and-so. Well, you do. But here's a straight tip from a silly old so-and-so to a clever young so-and-so. I'm worried about you and Fundament." I deprecated. "Well, you ought to be, because he's vicious. If he finds out you tipped me off, he'll try to do you some harm professionally. He probably means to already if you turned him down."

"I did."

"Good. Want to know how to deal with Fundament? The complete insecticide?"

"Well, yes—but since he's batting for Our Side."

"That," said Sir Frank, "was strictly for the birds. Now look: this is now a medical consultation between us two, over the health of John Fossil-Fundament, understand? That makes what I'm going to tell you Hippocratic. Right?"

"In strict professional confidence," I said.

"In strict professional confidence. In public life, you know what he's like. In private life, I happen to know he's some unpleasant kind of nut case—a queer of some sort—you'd know all these things. I don't know what sort, but a nasty sort—Krafft-Ebing and all that: rapes corpses or sleeps with a Labrador retriever or something. I wouldn't know the details. If he was a poor devil in the gutter he'd be in prison for life. As he's a cabinet minister he's going to a psychiatrist—been under treatment for four years. Simpler to sew up his buttons—works better. Still: of course one doesn't throw a thing like that up at a man, particularly not the details. People say they can't really help it.

But *I don't think it would hurt if he knows that you know*—particularly if he doesn't know exactly how much you do know. Now—I suggest this line of therapy. Take it down, Goggins. The man he's seeing is Hartwigg, Dr. Hartwigg. He's really a head-shrinker, of course, but he specializes in sex—one of these Freudian chaps. Write and tell Fundament that you've seen me —don't say what you told me, but tell him that I've suggested that if he still wants a sex expert he should ask Hartwigg, because you understand he knows him. All right? All perfectly clean and decent? Or don't you like it?"

I didn't much. All it meant was that I was damn sorry for Fundament and stopped being hostile to him personally. He made sense, as Chandra had predicted, and I felt my wish to abolish him punctured. Then I remembered he'd got live ammunition. We had to do something about the conference. And Sir Frank's idea seemed necessary, simply in self-defense, seeing how vulnerable I was going to be. I thanked him and left him there with more milk, this time with soda, cursing Pybus.

Altogether I wasn't displeased with the afternoon's work.

By the time I got back to the place where I had left Dulcinea we still had about half an hour left for the beach. Dulcinea said nothing—in the sun she was a solid ingot of contentment; I settled to reading. Finally she said, "What's that you're reading? Is it Chinese?"

I told her it was Sanskrit. Dulcinea said it looked like a thunderstorm. I worked that out.

"Nagari letters are flat at the top—clouds are flat at the bottom."

"Thunderclouds are flat at the top *and* bottom," said Dulcinea. "It looks very black." She rubbed the sand off her back and came alongside.

"Is that all one word?"

She'd got a pretty, thin finger.

"Yes and no—they join up: like Dutch trolleys."

"What is it?"

"This is a play."

"Read some out to me. Go on. I want to hear it."

I read her the passage from the *Malavagnimitra* which seemed to chime with her remarks about meteorology—where Iravati catches her man with a rival and belts him, literally with her gold waist ribbon—"like a flash of lightning out of a dark-eyed, weeping cloud."

"Mind you, it isn't a precedent," I told her. "Iravati was a queen and she'd been drinking."

"So you *can* read it," said Dulcinea, slowly. The surprise was quite real. She thought that I had been sitting in front of it for twenty-five minutes beside a pretty girl who was almost naked, on a beach, on the Riviera, out of sheer lifemanship.

I was still only just finding out what a difficult past she must have had: I wondered who had tried so pathetically to impress her.

Little by little I was learning the full Otto story: more of it came out that night in bed, when it was too hot to sleep. They started letting off fireworks over the bay, and we sat there a little in the dark, skin to skin, watching them, shut in, as we had been in the lift going up to our first night together. That seemed much more than four days and five nights ago. In five nights we already knew our way round each other's bodies, but not round each other's minds.

I didn't ask Dulcinea any questions, on principle. It was she who started to explain of her own accord, as I had sensed that she would.

"You wanted to know about my being married to Otto."

She was finding it easier to talk in the dark, when I couldn't watch her—just as she always looked slightly above, not at me. This refusal of a straight look was nothing to do with evasiveness: it was more a form of privacy, which she now had to guard very carefully to keep herself from being trodden bare—it was "Keep off the grass." She had not let me into that garden yet.

"Well, I once said you didn't look married to him—but I know you are. Or aren't you?"

"Yes and no. I think it's no, but it could be yes. It depends whether he was telling the truth."

"I hope it's no."

"Otto was married already—he told me that much. And he said he was free now. But he's told me three separate stories. Most of the time she's been dead, but once he said he was divorced from her, thought he hadn't got any papers. And once he said that he thought she was alive, but she'd been under age, and he'd had to leave the country once before to avoid getting jailed for a false declaration."

"You could find out."

"By post? I can't go back to Hungary—if I'd wanted. And also I don't want . . ."

"To draw attention to us?"

"If you like. I think I'm just—tired; I don't want to go on thinking about Otto. And then if we are married—oh, damn! Why can't it be simple?"

I told her it was simple, as simple as our own compact, which had made itself without our permission and without any need of words. Our mental executives had arranged the thing for us like matchmaking relatives while we sat in an omnibus and talked about castles. It could go on being as simple as that, where I was concerned.

"You don't mind if we aren't married?"

I told her that I only minded if she did—if she wanted a dog license from God or the government and that made her happier I would give her one with pleasure, assuming that it could be done, but as I didn't care much for either licensing authority it would only bother me if she was bothered.

"I don't want a dog license," she said, "as you call it—but it's only if . . . well, without one it's not sinful or anything but it's temporary; like being on probation. I've always been on probation and temporary. If we'd got the silly piece of paper . . ."

She'd seen the way I picked her off Otto's finger. She was brooding—waiting for me to do it again with someone else. So I told her, very gently, "Your piece of paper didn't stop you leaving Otto. As far as I'm concerned you're not temporary; as far as I'm concerned we're as married now as we'd ever be, if a college of archbishops and registrars-general pronounced us man and wife from under the bed at the critical moment. It wouldn't make a ha'porth of difference saying 'till death do us part.'"

"Or till you find," said Dulcinea, "that you could get some interesting biological information from a midget, or a Hottentot with giant buttocks. I still think you're a nice person."

" 'Not a swine' was what you actually said."

"The nicest person who's ever . . . talked to me so long. But you're so ruthlessly enthusiastic and so incredibly thick-skinned. If you want a Hottentot to settle a point of interest I'll know I'm expendable. You'd call it completing the series; I'm learning the phrases."

With an arm well round her, palm down over her diaphragm, which was getting hiccoughy and unstable, I said that granted I might like to try a Hottentot, that did not mean leaving Dulcinea; and this applied to both of us so far as I was concerned, because there was no absolute rule now that one only dances with one's lifetime partner—though one may do just that for preference when she dances as beautifully as Dulcinea. She was in any event better off with an enthusiast with an intellectual interest than an ordinary husband with no insight, who went wenching to inflate his ego.

"I think," said Dulcinea, "a cerebral lecher could be worse, particularly when he thinks he's got what he calls 'insight.' He'd be single-minded, or he'd call it that. He'd go to hell over everyone's feelings to get a fact to stick in his beastly little book. You don't mean it, I know, but sometimes . . ."

"I'm matter of fact at the wrong time?" I suggested.

"No. It's like hammering on a tortoise to make it see."

"Right. Now listen," I said, "granted I'm not as perceptive as you want—in other words I can't predict your feelings. I can't predict anyone's feelings. That's why I couldn't be a psychiatrist—I can learn from study how people react, as I've learned about yam-giving ceremonies—I've learned what people are upset by. But I'm still being astounded by emotions they have which I simply don't share: jealousy, for example, or political patriotism, or the fear of being seen to be afraid. Possibly it's my handicap. It may well be pathological. But I want you to make me a promise. Don't do what all women I've ever known have tried to do. Don't insist that I must guess your feelings and then be furious when I get the wrong answer. Tell me. If you use words I'll understand them—nods and becks and wreathed smiles I won't. Human beings have tongues. They don't need to droop their shaggy ears and hope I shall understand."

"But I can't *put* them into words. I can't talk as you can. You never stop talking: you even verbalize the difference between my two breasts."

I told her that that was not difficult, and it was much harder to verbalize, for instance, the consequences of mood changes or how one felt.

"You're lecturing," she said, in the dark. She sounded like a small orphan.

"Well, promise one thing."

"What?"

"Help me this much. Have a whistle to blow when you see I'm not understanding, or to mean 'I want help.' You could do that."

"Yes. I think I could. Don't you want a whistle too?"

"No, because I'll tell you," I said. "On that basis we ought to be able to manage. Love starts below the navel and works up—what's fatal is to start it with a crop of unverbalized spiritual emotions and try to make some unfortunate person act them out for you."

I could hear her digesting this, unhopefully. Then she said, "I don't mind if you don't see, I will try to tell you things, and I don't care about forsaking all others, but don't forsake me." Her skin was wet all over, and I had failed to notice she was crying. I fitted her head on my bare shoulder—realizing that if she could only verbalize her feelings with difficulty she could express them physically with perfect clarity, and that this sort of proximity, short of actual coition, was the way to express my answers. I thought it better not to put this in words, in view of what had happened once before. At the same time I felt her getting gradually content. In ten minutes, during which I didn't speak, nor did she, she was wholly confident and relaxed. In twenty she was so near sleep I carried her to bed without disturbing her. Though I did not know it, this was actually a rehearsal. The conversation we had just finished, as well as the sequel, were to recur with a fairly strict premenstrual periodicity in each lunar month. On the twelfth or thirteenth postovulatory day I would begin to be lacking in comprehension and she would think about Otto. On the thirteenth or fourteenth the proximity method would be needed and would prove efficacious. If the Hindu work on this was all wasted by attaching the migrations of the Love God round the body of woman to the phase of the moon, not the hormones, at least they had the right idea. If I for my own part failed to anticipate feelings, at least I was going to be able to predict them.

Meanwhile, in my trouser pocket on the chair by the bed there was a letter of warm commendation for my project, and confirmation of my good character, from the Chief Inspector of Pelvic Organs to the Establishment, retired, which I'd obtained without cost or subterfuge. As for dishing Fundament's conference, it only remained to find time next day, after we had finished late French breakfast among the pots of oleander plants on the terrace, to write to Pybus and ask him some simple question which would send him trumpeting up to the Foreign Office to demand why he hadn't been consulted. The official denials would prove my point, and after that Fundament would be unable to get any cooperation from Pybus, or Sir Frank, or any of their immediate understrappers who had an eye to the succession. That would cover most of the amenable experts. I also took Sir Frank's advice and dropped a line to Fundament, inviting him to get the opinion of Dr. Hartwigg if he had any similar business to transact. It was a shot in the dark, but knowing Sir Frank I reckoned it would be worth the bullet. And I went to sleep interviewing Fundament and promising him a radical cure of behavior disorder, tailor's dummy syndrome, cabinet ministership, and all in one fundamental *therapia magna sterilans.*

The first step, on getting back to Paris, was to see Chandra about the classes. I wanted to make sure that there were no theoretical objections that I had failed to see; I wanted to be able to shunt disturbed applicants to his clinic, or at least get rid of them, and I wanted to plan our line of attack. Dulcinea, I'd found, though she was cooperative, or more accurately resigned, would hardly say a word in discussion of our joint approach to the pupils.

"After all," I warned her, "you'll be face to face with them in about a fortnight if we're lucky. You'll have to say something to them beside 'yes' and 'no,' which is what you've been saying to me whenever I've raised the matter. It may be my speciality, but it's your technique—are you coming to be there when I talk to Chandra?"

"You know," said Dulcinea, "you frighten me. You go about a lunatic project like this as if it were—as if it were real. I've said I'll help you. But do we have to take all the planning and the theory and the ifs and buts seriously—can't you just do the thing with your tongue in your cheek, please? Then you wouldn't feel you've got to kid me, and kid yourself, as well as the people we're supposed to be kidding."

It was amazing how this idea that I wasn't genuine had taken root, in spite of our very happy relationship. I had to remind her repeatedly that I wasn't Otto.

"Otto was easier," she said, *"he* ran clinics, and I had to help him, but he didn't talk seriously about it off duty. And make me discuss it—as if it was science."

I didn't press it. Her talents were practical. I was sure she would be all right once she was in contact with people. Once or twice during some of our own more intimate moments I tried to get her to verbalize what she was doing, but this only seemed to exasperate her, so I let her go her own way, and slipped out as soon as she fell asleep to tape-record notes on the actual techniques she'd used. In this way I'd have them for her when she came to need them in teaching.

I put the thing to Chandra in roughly the form I had first outlined it to Dulcinea. He had a longish think about it. Then he said, "Well, in my culture, of course, it's always been traditionally regarded as a good thing to teach like this—not at classes, of course, but in words and pictures. Peddlers sell them, and instruct even the illiterate. I can't see any harm it will do in your culture. But you reverse the priorities—you want to make them enjoy sex, then they will grow up into real people. But it is because they cannot grow up into real people they don't enjoy it. Try however, by all means."

I told him I'd tried before and it had usually worked.

"Perhaps, I concede, you will reverse the cultural part of their handicap. You tell them, go right ahead, Daddy Science says you can enjoy making love: right-ho, the outcome depends whether you will shout louder than Daddy Oedipus who told them that that was dirty and dangerous. For some it will work— but if they are queer you will not make them less queer simply by the classes."

"Any other objections?" I asked.

"The only other objection, you know, is yourself. You seem to be involved emotionally in this topic of study."

"You wouldn't think me a suitable person to run clinics, granting that?"

"Apart from the fact that you are as mad as a hatter, very suitable: nobody I think in your culture who was not involved and as mad as a hatter would start them. Press on, you are no worse than most other medical men."

We had had this argument a good many times before. It was inclined to end with Chandra arguing that my interest in women, and my habit of making my work and my leisure activities cover the same ground, were a compensation for latent homosexuality—this always struck me as a Freudian two-headed penny, though I see the force of it. I was waiting for him to quote the fact that the classes meant "lending" Dulcinea to other people as confirmatory evidence of this so that I could point out I was lending her exclusively to other women, to see what he made of that, but instead he remarked paternally, "You press on. I shall be interested—if I give you insight now I shall spoil the whole thing."

"You don't think I've got insight?"

"No, volubility."

"I went into medicine," I told him, severely, "out of an infantile curiosity about the difference between the sexes. Now I know the difference, the curiosity has become a permanent trait and I still like medicine. The superego fully approves the rationalization. My lack of social affect is a sign of immaturity, and largely defensive, but it's also bloody useful. My exaggerated interest in genitality—"

"You have learned this," said Chandra, genially, "by heart. I still think you are as mad as a hatter. While you are happy mad I have no reason to interfere, but only to caution you not to make other people pay too much."

I hadn't thought what the fee for the course would be. "How much would it be reasonable to ask them to pay?" I asked him. "We only want to live—I suppose about $75 or 20 guineas per brace per course would cover, if they'll wear it."

"I mean in your private life, metaphorically. This girl of yours, she is a person to be treated as a person, and the people you advise, these are not your new tin soldiers, you know."

For a moment I wonder if he had somehow been conspiring with Dulcinea to reform me—it was nice of them to try, and I took their point. I told Chandra so, and that I wasn't intentionally playing, either with Dulcinea or the people who came for advice—at least, not more than others, because human relations *are* largely play therapy anyhow. That set off an Indian reverie: "Who shall say how much play is earnest and how much earnest is unwilling play" and so forth, which held up business a little. But the interview had the concrete outcome that Chandra didn't see anything likely to go seriously wrong with the classes and thought them likely to do more good than harm, that he'd warn me if he thought I was mishandling them or doing anything crazy, and that he would see any genuinely disturbed applicants who couldn't safely be put through the course. At the same time he'd be able to send selected cases of his own who needed some support in getting heterosexual experience and I'd deal with them as he instructed. Most important of all, he could arrange me quarters for the classes—he had an old outpatient wing which had been nicely done up before he moved into a new building, and I could use that four half days a week when the staff interviews were not needing it.

It remained, now, to get the patients. I was to be the worm as well as the hook. I had to swim about in suitable waters until I had picked up enough hoverers and free-consultation seekers to make a quorum. Accordingly, instead of taking the chance to go for long walks on the quais with Dulcinea, to take her out to the places I knew, to go out to Charenton to see the barges, to do Versailles and the Musée d'Impressionisme, to talk to all the real people who built Paris as a place to live in, who fill the buses and the streets, and who would have found my classes the best music hall turn since King Képi the Impossible tried to prosecute Sartre—instead of all this, I had to stay in the shopwindow, walking slowly among the stuffed figures at Friworld occasions and through successive Friworld window displays, like a tart doing the boulevard on the wrong side of the glass. Another side of Dulcinea came out in this tiresome business which she couldn't share by accompanying me: she took her own initiatives and was unbelievably efficient, unbelievably brisk over it. She would wake me in the morning with typewritten lists.

"Here's a list of all the Anglo-American parties this week which you could talk your way into, and these are the hostesses's names and phone numbers," or "Here's a list of scientific meetings where you might get picked up and invited out," and even "I've got some names of people on the Friworld staff who aren't supposed to be getting on with their wives . . ."

"Where on earth did you get that?" I asked.

"The press boys. I went into the Press Club and just sat."

"But have you got a press card?"

"No—but nobody asked me."

"But if they had asked you . . ."

"I'd have said I worked for the *Barrackpore Times*. You left an old copy in the bottom of your trunk." She poured me coffee. "There you are. It's sugared already."

Evidently she'd done this kind of thing for Otto. I went out of my way to stress my appreciation—and then warned her to stay away from the Press Club if she valued our lives and future income.

"But why?" she said. "If I'm a reporter I'm not news. Reporters are the one set of people nobody interviews." It was true. As soon as possible I rang Chandra and asked him to organize a press card for her.

I'd come in and hear her bright voice on the telephone, suddenly become plausibly, impeccably American: "Mrs. Ettinger? Hallo, Mamie! . . . Well, can't you guess? . . . No, it's me: Alice Saltonstal. . . . Well, you just think harder. . . . Yeah, it was. In Miami. . . . Now I'd only just heard you were here—can't we meet, since we're so close? . . . Oh dear—no, I'd just love to, but Thursday I can't. I have to *dance*—with Homer, you know. . . . No, I make *him*—exercise, Mamie, it's all that holds off his coronary—that's right, I tell him, I'm one samba away from widowhood. No, I wasn't inviting my own self—I wanted you to have the first chance at someone I have up my sleeve you just won't want to miss. Goggins. Dr. George Goggins! . . . Then where were you at college? George *Goggins*—the bi-ologist! . . . no, not germ warfare, sex, dear—sex! . . . Well, I heard that he *taught* Kinsey—And I thought, since you took up Zen—well, he's *been* in Asia, he's actually seen them. . . . That's just what I was going to try. I can't promise, but I'll try to get him for you. I'll try real hard, Mamie. I'll hold you to that, too—yeah, he's just sweet. And you know, since Homer talked to him—I shouldn't say it on the phone like this, but I've been a new woman. It feels like we were livin' in sin again. . . . He does, yeah, but he doesn't like talking about it. You have to draw him out. Of course you can! God bless, Mamie dear . . ." Then, seeing me—"That's Thursday night.

Eight thirty, just off the Rue Monsieur. Write it down. How do you like me as an American?"

I liked her. Three minutes later she'd be boss class plus. "Genocide Bureau? Extension two thousand two. Is that Mr. Tufthunter's secretary? I'm speaking for Dr. George Goggins. When *could* Mr. Tufthunter see him, I wonder? . . . Dr. George Goggins. . . . Well, *we* understand Mr. Tufthunter had asked to meet him. . . . If you'd just check. . . . Gone home? Oh dear, that's rather a blow! Well, look, do you think you could give me a provisional date. . . ? I'm afraid he may miss Dr. Goggins altogether if we can't fix something. I've got a great many engagements down for him, and he's just over from India, you know. I wondered if we could fit it in on Friday night? It would have to be after eight. . . . At a party? Well, it *might* be all right—I don't think he wanted to do more than make *contact*, you know. . . . Yes, I think that might be an answer. We will. We'll expect an invitation in the ordinary way. Thanks awfully. You've helped me out of a real *impasse*." She even had the post-athletic, hockey-over flush, which faded with the affected voice. "How did I do? That's Friday. At the Genocide Bureau."

In the past, hoverers had been a constant social embarrassment. Now, of course, when they were wanted, they were slow in coming—painfully, painfully slow. Eight Friworld parties to which we invited me in the first week, among them, yielded only three brace and a possible. I even began to wonder if I dare risk asking for the assistance of Boyo; but I knew what it would mean. Then a letter arrived from Cannes, a totally unsolicited and unexpected letter—

Dear Dr. Goggins,

Sir Frank has asked me to inquire whether, in the course of group therapy sessions which you mentioned to him, you would be able to accommodate a number of patients with marital problems who have recently consulted him, and whom he feels would be likely to benefit from the course.

If you have vacancies for these patients, I would be much obliged if you would let me know as they arise. Or, if you would find it more convenient, I will prepare a list so that you can communicate directly with them.

Sir Frank asks me to express once more his good wishes and his sense of obligation for the advice you so kindly gave him.

Signed, Martha Mills.

Mrs. M. Mills,
Secretary to Sir Frank Pus, F.R.C.S., F.R.C.O.G., K.C.V.O.

I wrote for the list, thankful that typescript is less liable to betray emotion than handwriting. On the list were forty-six names, all within easy reach of Paris—with the peculiar proviso that most of them wished to be registered pseudonymously. "I have given you the correct names in confidence," wrote Mrs. Martha, "owing to the confusion which might occur between the eighteen patients who gave the name of Jones. Perhaps you will be able to point this out to them, or to allocate numbers."

We decided to accept a dozen brace for the initial course, expecting to shed a sizable proportion in the two "stress" sessions with which I was proposing to start. All the time we were waiting for cases I was designing these very carefully, to make sure that we shed the irrevocably shockable without giving them anything to discuss publicly afterward. I had also tape-recorded three or four of the trickier later lectures so that they could be given *in absentia* to single couples (the cubicles in the clinic, by a stroke of superb luck, were meant for audiometry and were soundproof). I also spent a great deal of time in toyshops. I was looking for dummies which would be anatomically correct and would bend in the right places, but would not be much more mobile about the joints than the average Friworlder. As a test, I tried to sit them in the Buddha's posture of meditation, the siddhasana, which most Europeans can't quite manage without practice. Tests on the dolls in the Samaritaine excited far more notice than I'd imagined they would. Dulcinea, who was with me, saved this situation like lightning by telling the assistant we were going to use them to demonstrate yoga, which was true. It was she who found the right thing on a stall in the Rue St. Vincent—it was she who typed the bidding letters. D. F. McGredy (Miss) had Mrs. Martha beaten hollow. We had no office until the clinic was ready, so she typed them lying on her side with me on the bed at Robinson. I wondered if the recipients would ever come to lie like that in our species of contentment, or if Chandra was right in expecting them to be too immature instinctually for us to help them.

Then, the night before we were due to start, Dulcinea had a bad fit of nerves. I'd miscounted from the last occasion when I'd been lacking in consideration, but Otto and insecurity arrived on time in accordance with the Moon God's circumambulation. This time I knew how to deal with them, however.

At breakfast, before we left to get the premises ready for the patients, Dulcinea said, "I'm frightened," but she went on, "you will be there all the time, won't you?" which augured well, and then, matter of fact again, "I've got to get the vases and the flowers. I'll leave you when we get to Denfert-Rochereau."

I asked her if she'd join me before lunch.

"That depends if I've finished. But don't you be late— they'll all be nervous and they'll never forgive you if you're as casual with them . . ." She was going to have said "as you are with me," but I saw her remember last night's consolation and smile internally, and she kissed me instead with very reassuring affection, heel-off-ground, as if she wasn't worried about the lessons or anything else. I wished I wasn't.

Dulcinea had arranged a great vase of flowers in the passage. There was Chandra's secretary in a white overall to welcome the applicants and register them at a little table. Inside we'd made it a sherry party, not a clinic. Dulcinea's dress was a masterpiece. It was her own work, on the hotel maid's sewing machine. She had aimed at something smart and worldly but with the medical note, and all those suggestions were present—it was the soul of the classes manifest. The trick depended on a big box pleat. I got Dulcinea to "register" as a test run, and the stopwatch showed a two minute lag between the arrival of our people in the hall, where they had to register and hang up coats, and the announcement of their names at the door (the waiter was hired with the sherry glasses—he'd been warned about the high incidence of Joneses). Ten minutes before time, I could pick some of them out, pacing up and down or lurking in unlikely places as if they were waiting to intercept a bank cashier and help themselves to his bag. Gradually they closed in. The first couple went up to the door and back to the street gate three times, each journey getting shorter. It was exactly the behavior of wild sheep with an unfamiliar object. Then another couple came up at express speed, looking neither left nor right and were in through the door before it was properly open. Immediately all the others sauntered in, couples popping from ambush in cars and in front of shopwindows to form a rather unhappy little queue in the hall before the registration table.

Then the waiter bawled out, "MR. and MRS. JONES!" and we were off.

It was not my day. It was Dulcinea's day. They came in like dental cases or the newcomers to a VD clinic. Within minutes the cumulative atmosphere had become that of a dancing class. In the intervals of smiling and dignified conversation I couldn't help assessing them as material. They were of all shapes and sizes. Some of these combinations looked barely workable. The subjects were all subboss-class English or Nato-Americanoids. Most of the women were shrill—there wasn't one plushy, satisfied voice. The men were assorted, but I could pick out three or four early, and one very bad, case of the tailor's dummy syndrome. I had to take care not to ask the severest which constituency he represented. On any normal occasion they must have formed a poor impression of my own state of relaxed confidence, but they were so afraid of me, the man who was going to ask questions and embarrass them and reveal their hidden deficiencies, that nothing else mattered. Yet among this Dulcinea shone. Gradually as she moved round we had chattering, then laughter, finally babel as the sherry moved in. She was carrying the whole occasion.

Finally the party began to form itself into a long horse-shoe round me, the waiter took the glasses and shut the doors, and we were due to start business. Our first crisis came at that moment. I was moving a very tall American with a midget wife back under starters' orders; he was talking all the way out of sheer apprehension, and I was reckoning up the chances that when the course was over that couple would be adjusted to the *sthīta-bandha* techniques which seemed the only way of getting mechanical coaptation, when there was a silence—the kind that makes the Russians say that a little policeman is being born. In the middle of this, my American bellowed to Dulcinea, in a terrified falsetto, "You married to this gentleman?"

Dulcinea's face went out like a snuffed lamp. I saw her nails digging in. Fortunately she managed to speak before I could interfere. "No," she said, "I *am* married, of course, but I'm afraid I don't know where my husband is." Then, with a wonderful, spontaneous projection of love, anxiety, and shyness—"We think he may be in Hungary." Sympathy ran round the room like a little wind. Dulcinea, turning away from the pupils at the follow-through of her little gesture of longing, gave me a minute wink. The gate went up and the field was well away.

"Well, ladies and gentlemen," I said, "as I think you know you are all here with one object. You want to improve your sexual performance in marriage. Some of us I expect will have specific difficulties, with which we shall be dealing. The rest are probably just not convinced that they are getting the best out of an experience which is, after all, biologically designed to be one of the really rewarding things in life. Now I think you'll probably recognize already that your chief difficulty in dealing with this problem is reticence—the fact that in our culture we *are* reticent about these things. In fact, it's this reticence which has probably prevented you from seeking advice before. On any other subject you'd talk freely to your neighbors and find out how they manage things. Now, I'm going to begin these classes on the understanding that this reticence has been overcome. We have to be able to discuss the whole field exactly as we'd discuss (I tried to gauge the Anglo-American percentages) "the care of lawns, or the choice of an automobile."

We went on to the lack of vocabulary, the fact that we'd have to correct popular ideas of what was normal—this drew a hoarse cry from the man who'd questioned Dulcinea, "We know Kinsey!"—and we'd have to realize that sexual enjoyment was a skill. Like ballroom dancing. In every sense like ballroom dancing. I saw a cloud go over half a dozen faces as I said this, and I saw Dulcinea dispel it by looking straight back at them with a radiant, tropical smile. I rammed the Terpsichorean argument down a little. Then I said, "Let's sit down to it." I'd reckoned the pause while the stacking chairs were passed out, which I'd timed at seventy to eighty seconds, was about right to let them get their breath. Once they were settled I outlined what we were going to do. Initially we'd discuss the subject in general, with questions. That would cover two sessions. Next we'd split the class and Dulcinea and I would talk to women and men separately. Later we would recombine. "Now you realize," I said, "that in order to learn to do something, you've obviously got to do it. I want to make it clear that there will be no public instruction here which infringes the privacy of our individual married lives, but certain exercises are essential. I want you to take our word for it that we will see that these are conducted in a way which won't embarrass or distress you—*that* is why we're *here*. Then there is the fact that in our society, as you know, there is a very strong objection, even a distaste, for pictorial representations of coition. It's odd, if you think of it—here's something we do every day which most of you may never have seen in a picture. I think you'll see that for our purposes it may be necessary for us to overcome this unfamiliarity. If necessary, we will give you this kind of instruction individually so that you don't find it unpleasant."

As we went in deeper, I tried to spot the nonjumpers, but there was a room full of intent frowns. The stress passage had been written very carefully and memorized, with Chandra's advice, to pick out anyone who might be seriously disturbed by the main ancillary techniques we were to teach them. Dulcinea had stopped looking at the class and was looking at me. I could feel the cucumber-cool interest on her face carrying the waverers over the things that might have upset them. It was time for questions. I invited them. Nobody spoke. The clock ticked like a bomb. Then a not very cultured female English voice said, "I've never had—that experience, once. It is so good to hear someone talking sensibly about all this"— and we were there. Questions poured in—whether it really was a matter of skill, weren't we overrating the need for diversity, could we explain why, how is it that we can't, is it true that some people. . . ? I stopped them when we had overrun by twenty minutes. I could see the janitor looking in. "Now that we know each other, we'll meet again here on Friday," I said. "I want to make it clear, of course, that if you don't feel that the classes are likely to help you, or if you find them in any way distasteful, you can withdraw without any obligation. Personally I hope you won't, but if you decide to do so I'd be most grateful if you'd let me know."

We had one castaway at once. He was sure the courses would help him, but didn't feel that he could expect his wife to listen to this sort of thing. He was sure it was medically excellent, but she hadn't been quite used to that style of discussion, and therefore . . . The look on the wife's face didn't bear this out, but we wished him a very polite good-day.

Dulcinea was rather silent. I could see virtue had gone out of her. In the train she said, "I thought it was going to be horrid." There was a pause of nearly a station. Then she finished off the remark. "It's not a bit horrid, George, I *like* the people. And we really *can* help them."

"Is it real?" I asked her.

"We'll make it real."

The success had been hers entirely.

As soon as the classes were safely established, I was able to resume serious research and start work in the room they'd given me at the institute. This was first class in every respect apart from the truly diabolical noise of the air compressors in the next room. I had to tolerate these to begin with—at least until I'd seen how often they were in use. For the first two days they ran continuously the whole time I was in the building, and, from what I could gather, all night as well. On the third day, halfway through the afternoon, they suddenly cut out. The noise ran slowly down the scale from a whistle to a growl and stopped, leaving a blank space. I was hoping that the preparation was over, and my neighbor had switched off— or that he'd got fed up with the noise himself and decided to take a holiday from it—but there was a stampede and a carry-ing-on next door which suggested that the stoppage was un-intentional. I could hear doors slamming, windows being opened, and a head came round my door—"Attention! Ouvrez les fenêtres! Sortez pas!" It was gone before I could question it. I had heard flaps like this before in many laboratories; they are part of the occasional scenery of research, like ether fires and blocked pipes and they are rarely very serious. My door looked pretty gas-tight, so I carried on, sniffing at ten second intervals, with the fire escape door open in case I had to evac-uate.

I didn't smell any of the usual things, however, or, in fact, anything. My neighbor got the fans restarted in about ten minutes, after cutting my power and lights off several times in search of his own room fuses, and I heard him shut his windows, so I shut mine. After about ten minutes I had for-gotten the whole thing, when I suddenly found myself thinking vividly about Dulcinea—embarrassingly so, to an extent I found hard to explain. I had an impression that she was there, or some woman was there, and not only there but excited. This came and went again like an aura. It was a pleasant enough sensation, but just too vivid to be right. It took a few moments of thought to realize that it was a perfume, which was getting stronger and stronger: chiefly tuberose, so far as I could judge: not only was there an invisible woman just behind me, but I remembered India and the flower garlands; in fact, with that whiff of tuberose I was momentarily *in* India. There was more to it than flowers, however. There was a grassy, mealy undertone that produced a mental click like a change of gear. I couldn't identify the chemical. It was none of the ordinary laboratory hazards. I opened the fire escape door again and actually went outside on the perforated metal landing at the top, just in case this strange, active smell was something toxic, but I wasn't wobbly or hallucinated. I could just smell flowers and woman—that was all. When I went back into the room the same thing happened again. After a few moments I saturated and couldn't smell it anymore. There were no further developments, except that I went on feeling affectionate. The blotter felt feminine. It wanted to be stroked. So did my own knee.

At that moment my first batch of human spermatozoa arrived and I had to start work, fumes or no fumes. I noticed that the little technician who brought them up looked flushed too, but she might have been embarrassed by the contents of the vacuum flask, and she'd run from the clinic, so that wasn't strange, and I couldn't waste time in speculating about smells while my specimens gradually gave up hope and died.

No sooner did I get inside our room at Robinson that night, than Dulcinea started to flush. Color spread upward from her chin to her temples.

"Ooh!" she said, "what's that?"

"What's what?"

"What have you been drinking? Or is it a chemical?"

I didn't follow her.

"The perfume! I thought for a moment you'd been with some woman. It *is* perfume, isn't it?"

I told her I thought it must be, since my neighbour was a perfume chemist and something had been escaping which he was very excited about.

"I can smell it," she said, "in your breath. It's nice! George . . ." She went on steadily flushing and started to sparkle.

Her mouth came open a little way. That was the complete Chartreuse syndrome.

"It had the same effect on me," I told her, undoing her hooks. "I wonder what it is."

"I don't really mind," she said "what it is."

There can't have been much of the stuff on me, but it attached itself to Dulcinea, to what she already had, to her personality—we seemed to be covered with it. In fact we'd barely rested five minutes when it reasserted itself.

Even then, the memory lingered on. It still wasn't satisfied. Dulcinea got up.

"We must wash this off," she said, matter-of-factly, "or we'll be here for the rest of our lives." Her resolution still persisted when she found there wasn't any water in either tap. "We'll wash downstairs. Come down with me."

"After," I said. I was still sleepy.

"No, *with* me. There's an enormous dog."

"Where? In the washroom?"

"No, outside. It stands in the passage. It got outside the toilet this morning and wouldn't let me out. It's a spiteful-looking dog and it's only got one eye."

"Then come out on its blind side," I said, turning face down and enjoying Dulcinea and tuberose and je-ne-sais-quoi, which still filled the room.

"Come with me; please—it says '*chien méchant*' outside the front door."

She pulled me off the bed by the foot, so I dressed and came after her.

"It's there," she called back, from the stairs. It was, too—a nasty-looking animal, very old, too big to fool with, and obviously mean.

"The simplest thing," I said, "is to call the barman. I'm not moving other people's *chiens méchants*." To do that, however, I had to pass in front of Cerberus's nose: there was a loose stair banister which came out in one's hand. I slipped this out as nonchalantly as possible, so as to have something I could shut Cerberus's good eye with if he lived up to his appearance, and went up to him. I could see damn well that his intentions weren't honorable. He had the same idea about me. Dulcinea called to me to come back. Cerberus rolled up his lip and showed a grin full of septic teeth like a cottage piano. Then he must have breathed in, because he got my wind. He suddenly bristled from head to tail. The meanness in his eye went out like a match, and he fled with an extraordinarily undoglike howl. I could hear him howling and scrabbling at the back door to get out. So could the barman. He came out inconveniently soon and saw me putting back the banister. He went down to get the dog, saying something about my being an imbecile and the dog not supporting blows with a stick. When he found he couldn't drag the animal past me by main force, he said I must have it *"brutalisé,"* and obviously didn't believe denials.

I was much more interested than put out. I hadn't hit the dog and I was quite certain that what had hit it wasn't the sight of a piece of one-by-one in my hand—it was the perfume. The creature bolted from Dulcinea in exactly the same way when she met it later that night. As for our room, the atmosphere was still stimulating when we went to bed, and even with the windows open it stayed like that until well on into the early morning.

I meant to catch my neighbor next day and find out what was going on, but he forestalled me. I knew he was a small, dark young man with a slug moustache and very shiny hair—Sir Frank would undoubtedly have called him the perfume type. He had a little gold lapel badge in the shape of a hexagon

—presumably it stood for a benzene ring and belonged to a chemical club. When I went to lunch he was lying in wait for me.

"*Excusez, monsieur. Vous permettez que je me presente? Pierre Marcel. Enchanté. Et c'est vous Dr. Goggins? Vous travaillez sur les problèmes de comportement sexuel humain? Je ne vous dérange pas? Parce que j'ai plusieurs questions que . . ."*

No, I thought, no—not this one too. *Çe ne biche pas avec sa femme.*

". . . because I'm working in the same field myself. I feel I know you already from your published work," he went on. He caught my eye. "Its all right—I'm not impotent. I'm not a queer, my wife isn't leaving me, because I'm not married; in other words, I don't want a free consultation. I just want to talk research." He grinned at my relief. "I can see you've had some too," he said.

From that moment we understood each other perfectly.

"I must get your advice," Marcel was saying, all the way down the Rue St. Jacques, "let's go somewhere quiet because I don't want to be overheard. In here . . ." I followed him without objection. The place seemed to fill the bill for a confidential research conference. We settled down, and out it all came in a flood.

"I've got to tell you—first because I'm onto something I can't handle myself (I've been waiting for you to get here—it's been ages, you can see how impatient I am) and secondly because you know about it already after yesterday. In fact, I'd have told you yesterday, but I couldn't go out of the lab, I didn't like to trust myself in the street in view of what has happened with the smaller quantities: did you notice anything? You must have, you're a trained observer. I'll have to begin," he started eating the soup which had been brought, unordered, without ceasing to talk, "at the beginning. Forgive me if I tell you what you know. Listen carefully." He dipped his finger in the soup and drew a diagram on the tabletop. "This is civetone. I chose it as my starting point because it is known to have these

effects, and it resembles in outline the mammalian sex hormones . . .

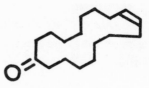

From this . . ."

"Stop," I said.

"I set about preparing the other cyclic compounds, those,
you understand, which . . ."

"Stop," I said.

". . . in any case I'd have to work my way through several
hundred . . ."

I pointed a bread baton at his heart and shouted, "Halt,
or I fire."

"I'm sorry," said Marcel. "I've been waiting three months,
you know.

"I only want," I said, "to be sure I'm with you. I think I am.
I think I'm filling in what you haven't said. You are a perfume
chemist. You are looking into the effect of perfumes on human
sexual assortation. Starting from civetone you've got a real
beauty, and you've stumbled on a good deal more than you
bargained for."

"No! No, I have found exactly what I thought I would
find."

"Then presumably you were trying," I said, "to find a specific aphrodisiac which would act on man like the signal odors
of most other mammals."

"It was you who suggested this," said Marcel, and he
pointed the bread at me in return—"*J. hum. Sex and Reprod.
Behav.* 1964, page 88."

Now and then I have been hit below the belt by a sense
of responsibility for expressing any idea in print. Often it looks
as if nobody is influenced by printed matter of any kind, and

particularly by rational argument. Every few years, something happens to prove that every written opinion one does express is like a rifle shot fired into a thicket—you find a buck or a body. I hadn't forgotten this paper—but this torrent of words had the reference by heart, pinned to his brain like a phylactery, and my guess—made originally where all guesses of this sort are made, in a Common-Room argument over morning coffee—had been seething inside him ever since.

I even remember the argument. Someone had been talking about a recent improbable marriage between colleagues not then present, and we'd gone on to the matter of "imprinting"— whether the baby "learns" his future destined sex object by building in an attribute of his own parent. We talked about studies which people were making to see if wives resembled their husbands' mothers in appearance, and then about the difficulty of scoring the factors of likeness which might be involved. Since the process of fixing might happen early, and babies don't see clearly for some time after birth, we were arguing that voice might be more important, and then that smell and taste came first. Somebody quoted Groddeck's idea that "in marriage we let our noses choose for us," and that man's olfactory acuity is quite as great as the dog's if only he didn't repress it for psychosexual reasons—and from that I found myself arguing that it ought to be possible, starting from normal skin constituents, to produce substances which would act like long-range hormones, or the signal odors of animals which trigger off compulsive responses—fighting, mating, fear, and so on—and that these might easily act at such low levels that we wouldn't be aware what was hitting us. On reflection I quite liked the argument. It happened that an insatiable American conference was after me for one of those general speculations on the contribution of biology to psychology, psychology to biology, and one or both to education, faith, hope, charity, or some other variable. To write them a serious paper would be a waste of time—to refuse would lose me a free ride to California by first-class steamer and air. Accordingly I gave them the coffee conversation, tidied a little, and developed. I was able to show that while the male sex hormones have a skeleton like this

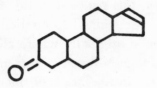

civetone, which makes civets think about other civets, makes men think about woman and goes into perfume as a "fixative," has a skeleton like this:

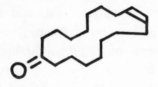

and that some of the sex hormones themselves have a pleasant odor in the crystalline state like perfumers' musk. And I worked the idea out a little from there. It would amuse the conference, give the press a "story" which would keep them from misreporting more serious scientific business (I could probably keep my name out on professional grounds), and save me having to think about a review article. This *jeu d'ésprit* was accepted—it earned me my fare and two double column headlines for the conference, which pleased the commercial sponsors greatly, even though they were—SEX MEN MEET: BRITON SLATES "CHEMICAL WEAPONS" FOR LOVERS, and SMELL ME, LOVE ME: PERFUME OF FUTURE SPELLS DOOM OF MALE: that had been all, so far as I was concerned.

As Marcel talked I felt decidedly humble. Evidently, and not for the first time, a jocular coffee speculation in the Common Room had turned out to be correct, and it had unloosed

some of the "strange repercussions" I'd flippantly catalogued
to the scientific peasantry of San Francisco—in fact, I had experienced some of them already—all in all it was a little alarming, but morally salutary.

Marcel was working for Francodor, the firm that has been
trying for years to beat the natural essential oils with its syn-
thetics. He was a dedicated man, for whom perfumes obviously
had a deep unconscious meaning, Groddeck or no Groddeck—
probably his mother was a broken flower, I thought; a tuberose
at least.

Fired by that infernal lecture, he'd started with civetone,
which was where I'd left off, and worked his way through a
forest of big-ring cycloketones. Apart from muscone, which was
already known, and things like exaltone, all of these had
smelled, but none smelled exciting. The most promising one
was a substance which came as an impurity in one of his syn-
theses. It appeared to be a double molecule—half was a cyclo-
pentadecanone, the other half was heterocyclic. "I was my own
experimental animal," said Marcel, "and this substance had an
effect on me. It might, of course, be suggestion. Now on theoretical grounds, as you know" (he knows, I thought, that I
don't, but he's telling me), "the odor should be enhanced by
acetylation. I accordingly made the derivative. It was quite,
quite odorless—as odorless as sugar. Misery! I can't do anymore
that day, so I go home. But I've been too hasty—I can't smell it,
but it is active as hell: dogs can smell it—they follow me—dogs
penetrate into the laboratory! The dirty old concièrge, not the
present one—asks finally if I am in season and can he have one
of the pups? I have to destroy the stuff quickly—the animal
house is in uproar—it can be heard all over the building. Two
months later a dog still comes in occasionally. Well, at least
we can send this to Australia for dingo bait, and there is something there. Like Pasteur I now have to ask myself, What? After
a great deal of thought I acetylate again, not here, on carbon 2,
but on carbon 3, here." He was half into my plate. My glass
went over. "Now the odor is back unequivocally. This time there

is no doubt. The theory of Goggins is vindicated. Within two hours I have had to dismiss a frustrated secretary, poor woman, for importunity—on the way home people behave peculiarly to me. Victory, then, at least in part."

It suddenly crossed my mind that Marcel was off his head. Women made advances to him. People whispered because he smelled. It would do for a delusion; then I remembered myself, and Dulcinea, and the dog. There was the other possibility, that he was both right *and* crazy. I filed that for future reference.

"Was that the stuff which got out yesterday?" I asked him.

"No, I am not there yet. Courage. In order, I set about acetylating each carbon in turn. I go round the molecule clockwise."

He counted on his fingers in my food—I had to eat round the demonstration of stereochemistry.

"One-acetyl, inactive: 2-acetyl, attracts dogs; 3-acetyl, active; 4-acetyl, nothing; 5-acetyl, active to about the same extent as 3-acetyl, with which I think it is also contaminated—the melting points are very close. But 6-acetyl is very active. It's monolactone also: I had got careless and inhaled a lot of it, and I practically lost interest in chemistry for a week. The sensation was pleasant, but I realize I must watch for dangers. I make next all the dilactones. They are inactive. This is not the road. So what then? I ask myself. I start on the diacetyl derivatives."

He looked rather alarmingly excited, I thought, and he'd a definite tremor of the fingers. I kept wondering, counting round the peas his sleeve had left on my plate, "Junkie, maniac, sane French scientist, addict, psychopath, con man, thief"?

"So far," said Marcel, "I have made two. Two only. The substance which you experienced was the 1, 3-diacetyl compound. You'll forgive me saying this breakdown was a lucky accident. This was the second batch I've made. And you've been able to judge if it's effective."

"How much got out yesterday?" I asked, "I mean, you

could avoid some of these crises if you made smaller amounts . . ."

He'd long since forgotten to eat his own meal, and I had lapped him by a course. He leaned over into my plate again.

"My friend, there was one milligram. Not all of that escaped. You see?"

I certainly did, and I whistled.

"But that isn't all," he continued. "We have a substance of quite formidable power. But everything suggests that the derivative which yet remains to be made, the 1, 6 diacetyl compound will be more active." I moved my plate out of the way of his dramatic sense.

"Enormously more active."

He was in the plate again with his sleeve nevertheless. I moved it further. "Any idea by what factor?" I said.

"By three, by four, by five orders of magnitude."

The plate went off the end of the table with a crash. The handful of other diners looked round, and the waiter came to retrieve the pieces.

"In that case," I said, "you'd better be damned careful with it. In the first place, don't make it in the institute, in the middle of Paris. Do it in a field . . ."

"My friend! I *am* careful. You don't need to warn me. I dare not make it at all. For three months I have been pausing and considering the implications of this work—the *wider* implications, you understand. I'm pretty well worn out with them. But I'm going to make it—that is not avoidable. The trouble is I've had nobody to consult. That's why I had to wait for your arrival. That's why I'm in a state of excitement. Nobody!"

"But surely . . ." He flapped me away.

"Nobody who had both the knowledge and a reasonable social attitude. Your opinions are known, and you've got both. Like me, you hate 'le règne des flics et des prêtres!' As I see it, we've got something here which belongs to mankind. If I consult the others, what will happen? What would have happened if Noah had consulted the High Priest and said, Look, I've invented alcohol—what shall I do with it? They'll say, Sell it, give it to the government, suppress it, give it to the CIA or the Russians, give it to the people who sell things, let the people who prohibit joy prohibit it. I say—Never on your life! And you'll say the same."

If he knew I'd say the same I was wondering why he'd waited in such agitation for my advice, but in general, and allowing for cross-cultural differences, I sympathized with his line of thought.

"Shall we let the crows get at it? Do we want the Pope at our heels? Listen, now they sell a car by printing a picture of it with a pretty girl—you buy the car, and you imagine you buy the girl. Now they will spray the car with the essence of desirability, and put it in the advertising ink. I say no! We have love in a bottle, we will let him out. *Écrasez l'infâme!* We will let out liberty, equality and . . . fraternity!"

I got him back across the table.

"You'll certainly let something out," I said, "probably your own patent right, if you go on shouting at the top of your voice in a public restaurant. Now listen, let's see what we really have got in the bottle. First, we have a substance which appears to be the first effective general aphrodisiac. It also scares dogs."

"You've noticed that? You are an observer who misses nothing."

"That," I said, "was the size of a barn door. What we haven't got is a shred of evidence that this stuff isn't toxic, addictive, or otherwise noxious."

"I am alive," said Marcel.

"Well, that may not last. Neither do we know what kind of response it produces in different people."

"I know," said Marcel, "that the effects differ. I will give you the facts in a minute, so far as I have them. Naturally they're incomplete."

"All right," I said. "So much for the stuff you have made. In addition—finish your entrée while I'm talking—we've also got a hypothetical substance which may be a great deal stronger. As you haven't made it, it may equally be a complete domino, or do something quite different—Pied-Pipe rats, or kill weeds. Let's deal with what we've got. Have you got a name for this stuff, to save breath?"

"It is not wise."

"No, not the chemical name—any old name, so that we can talk about it, instead of saying 1, 3 and 1, 6 diacetyl-thingummybob."

"It started as allumin, but that's confusing. I call it lascivin," said Marcel, " in my notes."

I pointed out that that gave the game away to any literate snooper and suggested he should call it something really irrelevant. He might, for example, call it 3-blindmycin.

"It is not of fungal origin," said Marcel.

"No, I know it isn't—but they all ran after the farmer's wife: reference to an English nursery rhyme—that should lead all unauthorized persons up the garden." I thought it was rather an apt choice.

In the time it took to explain this, he finished his entrée and became much calmer. I had had the crème caramel minutes before, and I cleared a space of crockery before going on with the discussion.

"All right, call it as you like," said Marcel, finally. "But there is another reason why I dare not make it. I have made the 1, 2 diacetyl compound."

"Which ought by analogy to attract dogs like the 2-compound, but a million times as much. Does it?"

"It has another action. I have not tried it on dogs. I'll show you later. I won't explain, if you don't mind, because I don't want to suggest my conclusion to you. Later."

He was quite determined not to say any more about that. "Now, you ask about the possible risks of the 1, 3-compound."

"You're quite sure," I said, "it hasn't hit you at all? You've been exposed for some time."

"Only pleasantly."

"You're quite sure," I said, "that it isn't cumulative? You

must realize you seem rather excited." He nodded. "You're aware of tension?"

"I am aware of tension all right, my friend. But it's not from the drug. It's from the weight of social responsibility we two now carry. I've carried it for months on my own."

"What about your own married life?"

"I am not married. I told you?"

"Married in its broad sense, sex life—I'm not married either."

"Only as it did yours. Only pleasantly. It caused me no embarrassment. I can't afford to marry—no French intellectual in my position can really pay for a wife. A group of us settled the problem operationally—you see this?"

He pointed to the little benzene hexagon in his buttonhole.

"This is the badge of the *Communauté des Six*—I have a sixth share in a librarian at the Institute of Paint Technology. This has worked excellently ever since we were students—we call ourselves the Benzene Ring; we're all chemists or medicals (that's a great safeguard from the health point of view). She's a witty girl and a graduate. The badge was her idea. I've had to tell her a little about the work—I couldn't really avoid it. She's kept observations for me . . . it's all right, she's not too interested and she isn't inquisitive."

"You're evidently assuming she won't get jealous one day and talk? I suppose you know. It strikes me that after all the hush-hush you've rather given hostages to fortune," I said. "Secrecy means you don't tell anyone, and a young woman in this situation . . ."

"Last of all. I know. But I had to. And there's no risk. Six is the ideal number, socially and operationally. We've worked it out as a rational problem—twenty-eight minus four divided by six gives us one day and one night appointment each per lunar month. There's no jealousy at all. But she noticed the stuff in any case; there was a carry-over to my other colleagues: it stayed in her breath for hours. I couldn't avoid some explanation."

I asked him if his own reaction had got less with time.

"No, I don't think so. It is just as pleasant as ever."

"You aren't, by any chance, becoming addicted? You ought to consider that."

"I have proof I am not," said Marcel, with dignity. "Each year we draw for her in vacation. I drew the lucky straw and took her to Biarritz for three weeks. All that time we were quite out of contact with chemicals. Everything was normal."

"And it hasn't exerted any important influence on your habits?"

"Only socially, and that's quite serious, as a matter of fact—apart from Minouche I'm a monk, I daren't mix with people anymore—women behave most foolishly. Sometimes I've thought of buying a second *lot* when one of the others goes— that would make me one-third proprietor. But we who use our heads, we must think of the ruinous loss of phosphate!" He looked as if he expected a compliment for being a martyr to the demands of asceticism.

"Bosh!" I said.

"Bosh? *Comment* bosh?"

I did him the favor of his life by telling him that the "ruinous loss of phosphate," as he ought to know, was less than a tablespoon of fertilizer a year, and that stud animals didn't die of dephosphatation.

"But it is in a medical book," he said. "That's where I read it. Didn't the oriental masters advise conservation for scholars?"

"It's still drivel."

"Oh." There was a pause. "Then when I can afford it I will revise my way of life. These ideas die very hard, don't they?" He finished the meal. Now the excitement was subsiding, he seemed a calculating type. "Really, though," Marcel went on, "the stuff doesn't affect my own behavior—never uncontrollably, at least. But on the other hand it does seem to affect some people much more. You'll think this unlikely, perhaps—I defer to your judgment; but I have the impression it acts much less controllably on the inhibited. It seems to give them liberal ideas, but as they aren't used to controlling themselves, as we uninhibited are, they make—well, pigs of themselves."

"What size series do you base it on?" I asked.

"Sorry, I can't particularize. One was a colleague at the institute, whom you may meet. But he made a pig of himself. Normally he is governed altogether by devout fear. The same with the concièrge—he's been dismissed, poor devil. You and I have always liberal opinions [the word was *libertin*] "and we're used to desiring women, but controlling ourselves and playing the game by the rules. The devout aren't. Twice, I see them upset very seriously, with consequences."

"That may be an extraordinarily important observation," I told him, "though it can't really be taken from two cases. It shouldn't be difficult to test."

"That's one reason I so badly wanted your advice."

"Now tell me one other thing," I said. "I take it Francodor are paying for all this."

"They are."

"And presumably expect some commercial return for their money."

"When I started this project," said Marcel, "I was only interested in getting them what they wanted. I've learned a great deal since. I shall decide what it's safe to give them."

"Will they go on paying out while you decide?"

"They've paid for five years."

"Presumably you'll have to give them something."

"I shall decide," said Marcel, "when we can see the larger perspective. It may be safe to give them one of the less active substances."

"Which will blow the thing wide open, enabling someone else to make the more active substances and claim the credit," I said. "How do you stand for publication?"

"Publication is entirely in my hands, luckily. Patent rights are theirs, however."

I told him I thought this was fortunate, because if the project were to leak, by far the best thing he could do would be to blow it wide open: at least nobody would then have a corner in the 3-blindmycinoids which they could abuse.

"And nobody can suppress them," said Marcel ferociously. "That's what people will try to do. But they won't be able. You say you don't know what these substances will do. Let me tell you what I think, and see if you laugh. I think they'll bring the Golden Age. Imagine living in a Poussin picture. In a world where they no longer say no. Come back with me now to the lab—all the time I've been telling you these marvels your English sangfroid has been stuffing itself with nourishment as if it hadn't a soul, but I'll surprise it yet. Come on, we don't want coffee."

I made him wait, on principle, while I drank it.

"You are a man I admire from your writing," he said, fidgeting. "You only pretend not to have a soul as an English pose; you come from the land of carbolic soap—all of them red-head, brunette, blonde, carbolic—like zabaglione and chicken and Chablis all trying to taste of nothing but mouthwash. It's a facet of conformity. That cup's empty—come on, my friend, come on!"

I had not previously realized quite how big Marcel's establishment was. So far as I'd seen he had only the room next to mine—in fact, his laboratory ran most of the way along the passage on my floor, and there was a little annex in the mezzanine round the corner, where several girls were working under heavy air conditioning, with an ozonizer crackling away in the middle of the ceiling. One of the technicians was sitting with both her arms in a beaker to the elbows, with a little stirrer running in the solvent between them. On the wall behind was a large card chart covered with little knots of human hair, redskin-scalp fashion.

"Acetone," said Marcel, pointing to the beaker lady, "getting out natural fixative." He pointed to the other wall, opposite the scalps, which had several curves on charts, as well as a couple of Siné's cartoon cats on postcards—"Hair pigment spectra."

"And the technicians," I said, as he bundled me along, "are

blonde, brunette, redhead-with-trichosiderin, redhead-without-trichosiderin, gingeroid, and near-albino."

"Precisely."

We were out of the other end of this room and round the corner into the next.

"I keep them well away from the other investigation. And they mustn't use perfume. That room is nasally 'soundproof.' Now here . . ."

We were skirting a kind of apothecary's shop screened off from the rest of the room by glass, leaving a passage.

". . . all the natural floral essences for test purposes. That's worth about a million francs, that green bottle—ylang-ylang: now here . . ."

There was no doubt about the perfume in this room. It was full of mouse cages in racks.

". . . oddly enough doesn't seem to contaminate them—I've even carried mice around in my pocket. But I've got two separate girls on these to be certain."

The next room, in semidarkness, contained a complete scaler system and a magnificent recording spectrophotometer, with the flat, white glare of the hydrogen lamp leaking out through the ventilation holes in the housing. The technician was an Asian girl.

"Annamite," said Marcel, without stopping, "they're special."

"Francodor have done you pretty well, haven't they?"

"Not badly at all. I've given them plenty for it, you know. Other things beside—the Goggins project; all the natural skin fixatives—only Francodor's products use them. I found methyl-squalene. . . . Come in; come in, what are you waiting for? Now, please, sit down. *Enfin!*"

This was the room next mine. The two enormous blowers were rigged up on gantries bolted to blocks in the floor. They were quiescent, or we should never have heard ourselves think. The whole of the middle of the room was occupied by a glass birdcage with shutters, air hoses, and a little bench inside it on which was a subsidiary glass cage equipped with remote handling tongs. As Marcel shut the door behind me I saw a notice on the outside of it:

DANGER DE MORT
LABO INTERDIT À MDLLES LES EMPLOYEES

accompanied by a skull and crossbones.

Keep out, danger of worse than death, I thought; I was glad I wasn't responsible for Marcel's staff, in view of the things he was making. It was more dangerous to virtue working here, even, than working for Boyo, whom they could at least see coming.

"Now, the 1, 2-compound," said Marcel, sitting on the other side of his little desk. "You are willing?"

"So long as it doesn't affect my judgment."

"There is no danger of any kind."

"Or make dogs follow me." I was thinking of the dog at Robinson.

"No danger, physical or social. I'm going to put the substance on my own skin. I only want you to record your response. But do exactly what I say: no questions, because I must not inculcate a prejudice before you try."

He put a little plastic handbasin between us and filled it from a Winchester. "One per cent citric acid," he explained. "To kill any excess. It acts instantly as a quench bath."

He took off his coat and rolled up his left sleeve. Then he fiddled about with something under the central fume cupboard, and I heard a safe door shut. Marcel came back with a green screw-top bottle. It appeared to be full of sherbet.

"More citric acid. As powder."

He fished out of the sherbet a small phial containing filter-paper strips half the size of a postage stamp, set it down, and took forceps from the drawer. Then he passed me a pencil and a pad of paper.

"This is the procedure," he said. "I will place a strip of paper on my skin here"—he indicated his forearm— "and the substance on male skin is slowly hydrolyzed. Traces are absorbed of the hydrolysate. No effect is produced on the wearer. What I want you to do is this. Raise your left hand . . ."

"And swear you're telling me the truth, the whole truth and nothing . . ."

"*Soyez sérieux, par example.* Raise your left hand and lower it as soon as you notice an effect of any kind upon yourself—mood, thinking, affections, anything."

"Agreed."

"Simultaneously write with your other hand some words describing me. Your reaction toward me, what I am like. Understood?"

"Just reassure me that in France a display of affection between male colleagues isn't a basis for lifelong blackmail," I said.

"There will be nothing of that kind."

He took out a slip of filter paper. "Now. Left hand up—write." He had his eye fixed on a stopwatch. After thirty seconds I lowered my hand.

"You feel something?"

"I feel a conviction that that was a blank run."

"Correct. On this filter paper there is nothing at all."

"I've written 'medium height, comes from Midi, voluble, must have a hell of a big research grant.'"

"Excellent. Now again." He took another slip. "Go!"

At ten seconds I'd written "short, dark, and handsome"—Marcel's forearm with its little postage stamp was under my nose. I wondered if he'd try two blanks to be sure and simultaneously began to resent the procedure. In fact I decided, quite suddenly, that I didn't really like this fellow; here was I wasting my time with a bloody little. . . . I clapped my left hand down quickly. Marcel, who'd had his eye on my face, put his arm in the bowl. The little stamp drifted off.

"*Hein?*" He looked hard at me.

That stab of furious, contemptuous anger at him had come on slowly enough for me to miss the change in my mood until it had developed, but the return to normal was a definite jolt.

"Yes?"

"I suddenly felt hopping mad with you. I wanted to call you something unforgivable."

Marcel nodded.

"Is that it?" I asked.

"Bitter resentment and jealousy—I am contemptible to you, I have stolen your umbrella: I have stolen your girl! Death to me?"

"More or less."

"What have you written?"

"It's probably something offensive. I don't mean it, you know—it isn't my considered . . ."

"No, no, of course, but let's see."

He took the paper and read out "short dark and handsome bloody conceited little—*qu'est-que-c'est que ce mot-ci?*"

"It's probably 'frog,'" I said, unhappily—"a derogatory name which Englishmen once used of the French."

He was delighted. "Frog, *c'est grenouille? Mais non, c'est encore trop long—regardez.*"

The word I had written was "OTTOPATH".

"Pathic, psychopath? Or perhaps osteopath—you are a doctor, and this is a deadly insult among doctors."

"Worse," I said. "And I know why I wrote OTTOPATH. There was someone else I didn't like whose name has got in."

"This substance," said Marcel, *con amore*, "is absorbed by the skin. In the female it is unchanged. In the male it is hydrolyzed and something is released—of great power. Some women say they can smell it—like cedarwood or cigar boxes. The wearer feels nothing. But *he excites the resentment of all other males.* Is this biologically possible?"

"It's not only possible," I said, slowly, "I've already got some reason to think that a substance of this kind exists in nature. In man. It would explain something—several things. Look, this stuff is dangerous; you may worry about 3-blind-mycin, but that could only start an orgy—this stuff is really open to abuse."

He was nodding like a happy Chinaman, delighted to see me looking shaken. "So you see why I am afraid to make your 3-blindmycin."

I told him I saw quite clearly, and I thought his hesitation was wise.

"We will make it, therefore, together. Under your supervision if you wish. After all, it is you who discovered the principle." We shook hands conscientiously.

"I had a very nasty series of experiences with this 1, 2-compound," said Marcel. "It took me a long time to realize what was happening. Incidentally, for this one I *have* got a name. It is cocuficin. It makes you feel as if you had been cuckolded. By the wearer. This describes the sensation accurately?"

I agreed that it did, but my mind was really on the word *ottopath* and the possibility that cocuficin, or cocuficinlike subliminal stimuli of other kinds, might make the cuckolding an active rather than a passive matter.

2
THE CAT AND
THE FIDDLE

A YEAR HAD GONE ALMOST BEFORE WE WERE
aware of it, a year spent between the laboratory, the classes,
the ruinously expensive flat near the Étoile to which we'd
moved to maintain the social tone of the project, and such
leisure as Dulcinea and I could snatch—walking in the woods
near Massy-Verrières, swimming when it was hot; dancing
when we got the chance, handicapped as we were by the big
difference between French ballroom habits and the compe-
tition style I was trying to teach to Dulcinea. We had very
little social life and made a rule never to meet pupils infor-
mally, but Marcel, Chandra, or both were almost permanent
residents, and we were constantly in conference, either over
the classes or over the progress of the experimental work.
Dulcinea would be crocheting or cooking throughout these
sessions, interjecting her strikingly wise remarks or her cups

of coffee. She had found her real vocation in the classes. It wasn't till Chandra pointed out the reason that I saw why they meant so much to her—"I think," said Chandra, "she makes other people's marriages stable and happy as a substitute perhaps for her own."

Not that we weren't happy. But even after a whole year she sometimes looked at me, when she thought I did not see, with the anxiety of an institutional child who expects to be deserted, and who doesn't dare to entertain any optimism. Our moments of security more than offset this, but it would clearly be some time before she was fully able to respond.

Marcel had been brought in on the classes by necessity—I spent too much time with him to be able to avoid the subject.

He listened to my account of them with a face of blank incomprehension, and said, "Evidently you are joking?" When I told him I was in frozen, sober earnest he said, "*Mille bordels!* You are exactly as you are depicted on the stage and in nineteenth-century fiction. Nobody but Anglo-Saxons could hold such classes, nobody but Anglo-Saxons could go to them." And he let off the first laugh I'd ever heard out of him, a rusty noise which hadn't been used for a long time. He was a painfully serious colleague. I didn't riposte about the Benzene Ring and the Gay Paree stereotype, because it would have been wasted. After a while, however, he too got interested in the classes, but I had a painful impression that he saw them as a potential field for pharmacological trials.

The synthetic work was going famously. More important, we were gradually finding out exactly what Marcel's stuff did to the human mind, from trials on some of Chandra's clinic patients who were actually undergoing analysis. "If it increases their libido," said Chandra, "it will probably only increase their symptoms. If, as you think, it affects the same sense of guilt, it may be highly beneficial." This was enough to justify the trial ethically, I thought. The result was most interesting. Chandra's guess was quite right. Sexual drive was quite certainly boosted, but at the same time the patients lost their sense of guilt almost completely, at least while the drug lasted.

This meant in practice (a) that Chandra could make them belch up half the repressed sources of that guilt in one large bubble, before the effect wore off, (b) that the effects on those who had learned to behave clubbably for reasons other than irrational fear weren't much more than they'd have got from three weeks' celibacy and a large Chartreuse, (c) but that those who hadn't, including a great many who had bought their morality in childhood at the usual suppliers, went unpredictably and delinquently gaga. Chandra, of course, had got them in hospital where this could be controlled, but it explained Marcel's unfortunate experiences with the two devout colleagues who'd inhaled the stuff. In small doses the effect was simply to give them a great sense of release and liberal opinions, but it was difficult to define a small dose, and there was no question of giving it to outpatients. Chandra was in heaven. He was like a child with a new toy—all kinds of motives and preoccupations which on Freudian grounds he'd regarded as sexual equivalents were being shown up by Marcel's smell to be just that. While the drug lasted, various patients quite lost interest in stamp collections, uniforms, political ideologies, even poetry. In fact only those who had acquired a rational as well as an unconscious motive for their interests kept them. "The doctor who, like you, Goggins, became a doctor through unconscious retention of infantile curiosities, through *voyeurism*, he will remain happily a doctor, since now he doctors for other satisfactions," Chandra explained. "The only nun who would stay a nun, by contrast, while inhaling this material, is she who is a hypocrite and has consciously become a nun for some social or material advantage —the sincere devotee's vocation becomes seen as a puff of irrelevance." For quite a while after that Dulcinea and I had a habit of describing things as puffs of irrelevance; it was one of Chandra's best phrases.

Clearly, in view of this we had to go ahead with the next derivative, the unknown quantity, "3-blindmycin" itself. In view of Marcel's hair-raising predictions of its activity we thought of making it somewhere outside Paris, but even then there would be the chance of a nasty surprise. In the end, at my instance, we compromised by making first not 3-blindmycin itself but its deoxy-derivative, the corresponding aldehyde, which should be much less active in the same direction. This would at least indicate whether the stuff attracted dogs, set people fighting, or excited pleasant thoughts—for all we knew it might turn out to be a good upper cylinder lubricant. We went ahead, therefore, with this synthesis, taking reasonable precautions as for a toxic chemical, and keeping a very close watch on everyone in contact with the intermediates as we made them.

We had completed three complete cycles of the classes and exhausted Sir Frank's list. Little by little we were gaining confidence. Our screening procedure was working. We shed about one-third of our applicants as a result of the two stress sessions—on the other hand, those who stayed were being transformed. Squeaky female voices went down like lifts—after three weeks many of the wives sounded as if they were being played at thirty-three instead of forty-five revolutions—the shrunken wattles turned to well-rounded necks, a typical postnuptial glow appeared which we called, for identification, Blake's sign—the lineaments of gratified desire. Blood began to flow in the limbs of the tailors' dummies, and flesh to replace wire and kapok. Pomposity leaked away, and people who had been born to govern, swank, and kick their neighbors around were happily unclothed and in their right minds, getting their first taste of Eden. I was greatly impressed by the extent of the change—it was even more striking than the effect of Marcel's smells, which were, after all, drugs—that simple instruction could do all this with so little experience to guide us.

By the time we had exhausted Sir Frank's postulants, and without any further humiliating touting, our book had begun to fill up with applicants. Silently, invisibly, we were taking them with a sigh. Nothing showed above the surface. In the course of the sessions we took the opportunity of enlisting gratitude to emphasize discretion—it was explained to pupils that any unwelcome publicity could easily destroy the venture, and they left us sworn to secrecy about the actual content of the courses: a pledge which so far as I know was never broken by a pupil who'd completed the session. On the other hand, they were to feel quite free to recommend us, and they did. The minor difficulties we'd anticipated had faded away as we reached them. The pupils had made no bones over using the Sanskrit names, for example, to designate techniques—the Oriental touch was a useful gimmick in itself, and within days they were chattering away about *daśanacchedya* and *aupariṣṭaka* like a congress of Orientalists. I'd considered Chinese, since the corresponding books are more practical, but transliterated the Chinese names were chichi in English—one couldn't sell a senior diplomat or a society hostess a technique called "the wild ducks flying on their backs" or "the plum blossom going under the railway bridge." There were naturally differences in physiological competence and in inclination, but the effects weren't worse than in any ordinary dancing class— all the pupils left us able to get some fun out of what they had learned, most were approaching bronze medal standard, and a few were up to silver medal standard or beyond and nearly ready for championship work and advanced techniques. In learning our own way, step by step with the pupils, we'd now reached the point of confidence at which we could experiment—with tape-recorded exercises for self-administration on the Linguaphone pattern; with a quick test for abnormal emphases based on a set of pictures clipped out of comic books and crime magazines, which we included in the screening test, and with group sessions for mutual criticism.

So far, we'd had strikingly little trouble from any of the expected quarters. Fundament had certainly not exploited his opportunities, and I had reason to think I knew why: little as I liked Sir Frank's valuable suggestion, there was every reason to think that without it I would have been figuring by then as a lecherous Russian agent with an ex-Iron-Curtain mistress corrupting morality and security fifty-fifty; or at least, if Fundament were clever enough not to make the smear campaign too strident, as someone "not wholly in sympathy with the Free World." A hint of this would have sent the Americans up the wall—as it was, even near-VIPs from the Friworld were appearing at the classes, and I had every reason to hope that in a few more months we would have so big a clientele in the machine itself that we would be out of danger.

Then there was Nobodaddy. The organ hadn't started playing once. The Protestant element was never unfriendly. As to the Papishes, I had made a rule at the start that we took no practicing Catholics; I imagined they would not come in any case, but to avoid any inquiry I wrote in advance to the nearest taboo-factory for an address to which we could send them. Any who did register were accordingly to be turned over by arrangement to a colleague, an unwholesome little celibate with egg down his soutane, who looked as if he'd been right through the elephant, and who'd been nominated by the Union Familiale and the Legion of Mary. I don't think we ever needed to use him.

The only wing I had failed to secure was the Left. In December, we suddenly found our classes filling the whole front page of L'Humanité. Their reporter had penetrated a sink of vice where the Friworld held not only secret orgies but actual classes in the farmyard behavior characteristic of decadent U.S. society, etc., etc. This was a shock, for we had had no previous press publicity whatever. What had happened was that one of the entrants eliminated at the second stress session of a previous course had been a leading English Marxist with a strong Kirk of Scotland background. As he had consequently not attended the rest of the course, he had no facts, but he was transferring his disappointment over his own disturbance to us, and he had a vivid Calvinist imagination, which was, unfortunately, in the main correct.

I had no anxiety over L'Humanité; the alarming thing was that the press at last were onto us. Papers started telephoning; it was evident that the next thing would be a feature in Paris-Match by someone who wasn't a Scotch Marxist and who'd taken the whole course. At the same time, I'd realized we could not hope to keep the press from hearing about the classes—it would be better to deal radically with them at the outset, and in spite of the readymade story we were sitting on I decided, after some thought, that it would not be too difficult.

Accordingly, I went the whole way. First I ostentatiously refused to answer any questions, to get them hopping. After twenty-four hours, before the story could leak, I arranged a full-scale press conference at the clinic on our class-free afternoon. It was essential to see that the whole press, including the agencies, got the treatment; I therefore had the cards marked "Whisky, sherry, apéritifs, and biscuits" to make sure they all came. When about two hundred had arrived, finished the drinks, and walked the biscuits into the carpet, I got them on chairs, mounted the rostrum, and began.

There were two main things to be done—the first was to poison the story, so that any future reference to the clinic and the classes would go straight on the spike unread: the second was to kill the other story they might find awkwardly interesting, namely, Dulcinea herself and her relations with me. In spite of her protests, I put my foot down about this— she had to be there on view, she had to receive the press with me, and she had to sit on the platform fully exposed; only she was to wear the clothes of an English moral welfare worker—gutter-brim hat, tin skirt, black boots. We couldn't get hold of these in France, even from the contractors who dressed the warders in women's prisons, but it proved well worth the expense of having them flown from London. We avoided the trite by not giving her spectacles, as she wanted— I was a little nervous that if we overdid it we should rouse suspicion. As it was, she was attractive still, but the idea of "relations" didn't enter one's head. There was no hope, so no story. The French photographers spent endless plates on the clothes, but that was what I wanted—the matter of our relationship was never raised.

The conference itself went according to plan. After three-quarters of an hour, half the two hundred starters had left, and most of the rest were looking at their watches. We'd been over the need for mutual forbearance, the exacting standard set by the Christian ideal of monogamy, the inherent dignity of the sexual impulse properly applied, and the beauty of self-control, and we were starting on the sacramental character of coition, even for those with no formal religious affiliation, when the evening papers went to bed. By then nobody was writing. After another ten minutes on the beauty of self-control *reprise*, the others decided there was no chance of any dirt now and scarpered. I could hear some of the Fleet Street contingent singing "The Lost Chord" in the passage, ending with a great Amen. The only member of the entire press corps who stuck it out and stayed to hear what we were actually teaching was a lady from a Mormon paper; I decided it wasn't quite suitable for her and told her so.

We got one report—in a paper for Swiss missionary candidates.

From then on, the freeze-up was complete and lasting. Every editor, French and English, killed any reference to the classes on sight, without bothering to read it, and we could have marched down the Boul' Mich' in the nude and not been reported. *L'Humanité* came back at us about every three months, but this, now I had taken precautions against a spill-over into the bourgeois press, was to our advantage—it ended any vestige of a chance that Fundament might smear me personally, and it acted as a certified *kashrut* with the Friworld. There was a statistically significant increase in American entrants almost at once. Little slips recommending us had started to circulate in the tea clubs and Ladies' Lincoln Leagues. And all the time, in spite of the absence of any conventional publicity, our ripples were spreading and spreading and making quite big ships fidget about and wish.

Soon after we reopened, following the Christmas recess, the registrants began to show a systematic trend. Dulcinea pointed it out first. "Have you noticed," she asked me, at the beginning of the second year of classes, "that we've got eight couples called Smith?" By the end of the course it had risen to sixteen. This was new—the Free World, for some reason, had always given their false names either as Jones or as John and Mary Doe, according to origin. At the same time I noticed there was now a row of Jags with G. B. plates and English registrations parked nose to tail outside the institute during business hours. The Smiths tended to have boss-class voices and thin, discontented, Ascotty wives, who fattened astonishingly during the course: among the men, there were some of the most advanced cases of TDS I had ever seen. I found that at least two brace of Smiths were flying over specially for each class, and back to London after it. Evidently someone top was singing our praises. Dulcinea was nervous about them and kept saying they were spying on us. I told her it was all according to plan—these were scouts, not spies, and it only meant that the wasps had found the honeypot; we must start an extra class on Saturdays for English commuters. I also put *The Field, Country Life,* and *The Illustrated London News* in the Group Discussion Room.

When the Saturday classes opened, the number of Smiths had risen to twenty-two brace. It did cross my mind that Boyo, or a journalist, could have identified most of them, but decided it wasn't Hippocratic or worth the risk of blackmail which was inseparable from anything that gave Boyo confidential information.

The next development, however, I hadn't expected, and it was much more interesting from the theoretical standpoint. Dulcinea had begun studying *The Illustrated London News* in the breaks between classes, and six months after the first batch of Smiths had qualified she spotted one of them among the jockeys and democratic Asian dictators on the dead-distinguished-divorced page, and brought it to show me.

"Isn't that one of ours?" she said.

It was one of the very earliest Smiths, a particularly severe case of TDS who had done extremely well. The initial struggle had been a sharp one, but he'd come through: we had seen him become gradually less waxy, his face had loosened, and when he left he was already able to talk in a natural voice—while his wife, who had been in a very bad way from living with an embalmed specimen, had opened like a rather squat bud. There he was—the picture shocked me, because the smirk and the suit were back as before, and it looked as if all our work had been wasted. Then I realized it was an old, pretreatment photograph. The caption said "The Under-Secretary of State for Military Refrigeration, Mr. George Alabaster, who has applied for the Chiltern Hundreds. He is to devote himself to cattle breeding."

One swallow doesn't make a summer, but by the time the second echelon of Smiths had been home a few weeks there had been a small shower of rather similar cases. They were shedding their prestige and getting into useful activities. Poodle-face, the Prime Minister—the Rt. Hon. Pontius Paradise, M.P.P.C., C.H, M.C., housemaid's knee and bar—had lost two P.P.L's, one to desert conservation in Israel and the other to digging his own garden. A small key arms firm in Leicester suddenly switched from missile parts to mouth organs—the managing director was a Smith who'd wandered in, quite by accident, when he and his wife had come over to Paris for a course of flattery at NATO headquarters. Dulcinea started cutting out the Smiths as they came to hand and pasting them in an album.

Chandra and I spent a lot of time trying to get at the theoretical basis of this. Neither of us had expected anything like such a radical effect on character structure. We could see two possible explanations—either the provision of a physiological form of regressive play-behavior was enabling all these Smiths to act out their behavior problems and discharge them, so that they stopped using public affairs for the purpose; or alternatively, and less probably, really frequent and prolonged orgasm might be having the same type of effect as electroshock —if so, this could well be what the Evolutionary Demon meant it to do, and we were onto a new, behavioral deficiency disease of fundamental importance. In any event, we were both impressed with the revolutionary implications of the pattern which seemed to be appearing.

At the same time, we were both deeply aware of our limitations. We could only help a minority of selected people. The turndown rate for the course was still anything up to fifty percent, made up of roughly equal numbers rejected on psychiatric grounds, and self-rejections who were shocked by the two initial stress sessions and walked out. At the same time our intake was already selected—the really seized-up characters would never even register. We'd never intended the project to have any wider sociopsychiatric value than this, and that still seemed to be true. "If only we could keep the other fifty percent," I said to Chandra, "it might begin to be important. If we motivate the stayers-away, it would be really revolutionary— we should have set out to teach a sport and ended by saving civilization; naturally it won't work."

"You still want to make them enjoy sex so they become psychosexually mature," said Chandra. "Instead you have to make them psychosexually mature so they enjoy sex—for this you must analyze them all."

"I know," I said. "Pity there isn't any shortcut."

"Has it occurred to you," said Chandra, "that the other half of this might be Marcel's stuff?"

As a matter of fact it had, but I didn't like to consider it. We were all right as we were. The risks seemed too big, and there was a vista of ethical implications stretching out of sight.

Chandra kept raising the idea each time we had a consultation. "It acts on the superego. We know roughly what it does. It would almost certainly keep the walkers-out from leaving the course. It can motivate people—even against their will, and it specifically removes the sense of guilt."

"It hits their superego but it doesn't clean up their id," I said. "Some of them might do on it, but given to people like Fossil-Fundament and Pontius Paradise it would probably motivate them to raise old Harry. That might not matter, but I'm not going to risk it on my patients."

"In small doses, in selected cases?" said Chandra.

"Suppose we do get them adjusted on it, how do we know it would last?" I said. "There might be a frightful reaction of guilt when the dose ran out."

"Maintenance therapy?"

"More likely addiction," I said.

I disclaim all responsibility for the first use of n-n deoxy-3-blindmycin in the institute, although in some sense I got the credit for the results. I still blame Chandra for the risk he took, and if I could blame Dulcinea for anything I'd blame her for being a party to it. Marcel, of course, would try anything he got fixed in his head. They waited until I had influenza—Chandra was taking my classes, and my nose was obstructed, or I'd have noticed that Dulcinea smelled not only of Dulcinea but of deoxy-3-blindmycin. The first I knew of it was when I saw Marcel furtively carrying a large box of soap down to the cold room. He'd turned off the cooling system. Inside, I found a hollow tower of little guest tablets of white castile soap, and a concentration of deoxy-3-blindmycin enough to affect my own self-control.

Chandra and Marcel were both positively defiant.

"We took no unnecessary risk," said Chandra. "All we did was to put soap tablets with a minute concentration of the stuff in the washroom at the clinic, and look at these figures!"

The walkout from the two stress lectures had fallen to zero. Not one Smith had been shocked.

I went through that course in agony, expecting at any minute that something would go wrong. It was the worst drug trial I ever remember. Chandra and Marcel were both flourishing—they wouldn't have to carry the can. I was even short with Dulcinea and told her that she'd endangered everything, including our plan for each other, by not telling me what was going on, but she seemed quite tranquil.

"I think it's rather nice," she said, "now I'm used to the perfume. I don't see how it could hurt anyone."

I kept a rigid control on Marcel's soap room. His technique was to expose two thousand tablets, which took hours to pile up, to 0.3 micrograms of the n-n deoxy compound on a piece of filter paper. He'd hung an enormous notice "RADIOACTIVITY —KEEP OUT" on the cold-room door, which was kept permanently locked for fear one of the girl technicians should go in. The big extractor fan was working reasonably well, and we were able to keep the stuff from impregnating our clothes. Eventually we used suits designed for handling tetraethyl lead, which were hot and uncomfortable but very effective. My big fear, that we'd get variation in the batches of soap, was fortunately not realized. We started tapering the dose well before the end of the course. By the time it finished, with 100 percent graduation, it seemed clear that the natural mechanisms had taken over, and there weren't going to be any withdrawal symptoms. The candidates were fantastically proficient and as happy as sandboys, and their Oedipal residues had been batted out of the ball park.

"There you are!" said Chandra. "Precisely as I told you."

Even at this stage I don't think any of us yet recognized the potency of the substances we were dealing with. The influx of Smiths, which we were able to handle with more and more confidence, and which got more and more interesting to follow, led eventually to a far more dangerous experiment that brought it home to us, but that wasn't just yet.

I hadn't forgotten Fundament and his conference, but the work at the institute, the classes, and Marcel's chemistry, to say nothing of Dulcinea off duty, made me lose count of the passage of time. Meanwhile Fundament, by a succession of stalling actions, had managed to get the discussion of tests put off time and again; in one way and another he'd managed to waste nearly two years, with the cooperation of the Russians, the Americans, and the other juvenile delinquents who didn't want their atomic switchblades confiscated. I had nobbled Sir Frank, and I was gratified to see that nobody else from the biological side, not even Pybus, had been willing to endorse the report. That left them with Cannon and Untergang, the ex-Nazi science-fiction merchant whom Fundament had to borrow from the Americans when even the AEC got too hot to hold him. I was waiting my chance to upset Fundament's applecart with these two as well, if I possibly could, but I saw no way to do it. Just at this stage, a new echelon of Smiths came in. Most of them were TDS cases—ten out of eleven—but the eleventh was Cannon.

It seemed beyond belief. Fortunately I hadn't shown any sign of recognition. He was accompanied by a little Manchester wife like a skinny Gracie Fields, a decent girl who had met Cannon when he was the star of the Tech, and was dead sick of being photographed with babies by Boyo's whitewash team each time her husband let off another atomic bomb. We discussed it in committee and examined every possible way in which Fundament might be behind Cannon's appearance at our classes, but Dulcinea, who had had a long talk with his wife, and was usually the most suspicious of us all, was satisfied that the application was genuine. Accordingly we agreed to take a calculated risk and devoted ourselves more intensively to the Cannons than to any other pair since the clinic opened.

The chief trouble at first was in getting Cannon to stop making flippant remarks and concentrate—he'd got so used to taking nothing seriously, as a defense against criticism of his employment, that he was difficult to approach at all. Once we were through the crust it was different. The schoolboy bravado, the big bangs, and the pride in his own ingenuity went with a terribly poor marital performance. Since the soap took care of the unconscious source of this, our past experience suggested that he would be fundamentally reconstructed if we could improve his game, and it was staggering to see how he matured as his anatomical equipment gained in reliability and stamina. Dulcinea, in whom Mrs. Cannon confided under a pledge of deadly secrecy, ran what I thought was a big risk in telling the wife straight out that if Smith-Cannon once got proper control and a sense of confidence in himself he'd lose all interest in rockets the size of the Washington Monument and bangs which abolished whole islands, but as usual Dulcinea's judgment was right, and Mrs. Cannon wanted nothing in the world better than that. After a short concentrated course, each afternoon during the fortnight that Cannon was hanging around in Paris, "consulting" with Fundament's minions about the forthcoming report, the result was striking. I was satisfied now that the Cannons' motives had been quite genuine: they'd been to a lot of trouble, it seemed, to dodge Cannon's own security officer—in fact, they came to the clinic through the back entry of the physics block, where the great man was supposed to be spending his afternoons in the library.

By then he could manage the four groups on a single stand, and his pride in the achievement was pathetic. His wife, who had got so sick of Cannon's technical genius and the bright-boy flattery which it got him that she went out of her way to be indifferent to it, was careful to show great enthusiasm and treat him as a virtuoso. At our last session Cannon shook hands like a dignified human being. I think he was on the verge of admitting his identity, but thought better of it. Mrs. Cannon's voice had started to get husky, and she was gaining weight. Dulcinea couldn't contain herself for impatience, and she didn't have long to wait. Three weeks later, with only five days to the conference, we heard he'd accepted the senior professorship of nuclear engineering in the University of the West Indies—ostensibly to study cosmic ray effects in the tropics—and Fundament was left to whistle for his second expert. That was two down, one to go.

We had a little dinner to celebrate Cannon's graduation as a *śastri* and a human being, at the Coq d'Or—with candles: Dulcinea at the head of the table as pleased as if she'd done it herself, Marcel, who put it down to the soap, and Tarunachandra, who kept going back to shop and thinking of extra reasons why the acquisition of full genital pleasure plus a few pregenital tricks should have as big an effect as a full analysis. By the end of the evening Dulcinea and Marcel had drunk toasts to me, themselves, Chandra, Cannon, Vātsyāyana, and Sigmund Freud, while Chandra and I drank soda and watched them getting progressively more uncritical. We'd adjourned onto the pavement, Dulcinea curled up like a kitten in a basket chair which completely engulfed her. Chandra had to go early

—it was extremely unfortunate that he did, because if he'd been there the subsequent conversation would have probably taken a different course. After toasting Freud they had got to drinking confusion to Fundament, then to Untergang.

"How do you say it in English—may God rot his guts, is it?" Marcel was asking me.

I was thinking about the conference more seriously just then and looking at the account of Cannon's defection in an evening paper a vendor had just brought round.

"I wish we could settle Untergang," I said. "There's a picture of him here, kissing a refugee baby. Pity we can't spray the swine with some of your cocuficin."

"We could do this?" said Marcel sitting up; I knew he'd never been quite reconciled to suppressing the stuff without seeing just what one could do with it.

I told him there wasn't a hope, unless he was willing to be caught, cocuficin and all—which would virtually hand the stuff over to the Pentagon.

"Please," said Dulcinea out of the chair, where we'd forgotten her, "what would it do to him?"

"It would make him decidedly unpopular," I said.

"If I smothered myself in whatever it's called and kissed him, would that do? I'm a refugee from tyranny—if he kisses babies he might kiss me. I'd try."

As usual, she'd got it. We could only listen, while Eve advertised the apple. She knew it all. Cocuficin doesn't take on women, so she'd run no risk. If the security men got nasty, she'd kiss them, and rely on cocuficin to stimulate the indignation of the bystanders. If anyone grabbed her, all adjacent males would set on him as soon as hydrolysis was complete, and she could slip out while they were fighting. "Please," she said, "can I try? It's bound to upset the conference at the very least, and what can we lose?"

"I've told you: it could hand over cocuficin to the Pentagon," I said.

"But how could they possibly find out?"

Being dead sober, I forbade it outright—apart from anything else, it wouldn't do the institute any good for her to be seen kissing Untergang. What was more, a lot of the Free World knew her. "Not with a different hair-do," she said, "men never do—even you didn't, remember? And if it works they'll have plenty of other things to put in the papers without printing me. If you like I can see the picture gets spoiled—I'll move: I'll—I'll make a face. So you must let me." She shut up her handbag, snap. What could we do?

And so, from a casual remark at a dinner party we were committed to the most dangerous experiment we ever undertook, though I didn't realize it. Next day we made concrete plans: or rather, Marcel and Dulcinea did. I was still sure they'd drop the idea before it came to the point. But I'd underrated Dulcinea badly.

We didn't go when the conference opened. I didn't want to remind Fossil-Fundament of my existence, and I wasn't interested in the evidence. Nor was the public. Fundament had stalled, very neatly, until the Tour de France was beginning. The attack by the neutrals of the world on the atomic powers was reported, but only in very small letters. On the second day the delegate of Ghana made the headlines by threatening an Africa-wide trade boycott if the fallout didn't stop, but as he attacked the French in particular all the later editions were seized. Nobody showed any great interest in the reason, but they were hopping mad to miss the sports page. Accordingly, when Fundament went in to bat next morning there was thunder in the air. He was the West's star turn—the Americans were keeping in the background, while the Russians were waiting until he'd jumped. Untergang was to follow in the afternoon. We were having our lunch in a café off the Rue d'Alger when Fundament's fat, democratic voice started coming out of the loudspeaker over our heads. I could see him and almost smell him—by that time I'd realized the risk we were running: that voice was the one thing that could have made me let Dulcinea go through with it. She was unruffled, cool as an ice cube, but I had to remind myself she wasn't really in much danger, whereas my institute was. Marcel kept getting on and off his

chair like a teething child, chucking cigarette ends right and
left—he was worrying about his cocuficin, not about Dulcinea—
and I wasn't much calmer, though at least I sat still. Fundament
finally overruled my better judgment. We finished our coffee.
"Now," said Dulcinea, "let's go." Then, because she knew the
state we were in, "It's going to be fun."

We'd dressed her as a Hungarian, under her raincoat—white
blouse and so on, with a national flag. We'd decided against a
bouquet for fear the bodyguard might question it. Chandra
had wangled her a diplomatic pass, so that Untergang couldn't
miss her. We weren't ourselves going in. As near the Élysée
Palace as possible she was to shed the coat, go a safe distance
from us and spray herself from a scent spray which Marcel had
in a sealed can, then march. She mustn't on any account push
against anybody—when it was over she mustn't stay to see the
result, but go straight back to the flat and get into a bath of
one percent citric acid, clothes and all. She repeated the briefing
solemnly, as if it were the shopping list. Then she kissed us
both, gave me the coat, and trotted off with the scent spray,
smoothing her hair as she went. When she was out of sight I
felt slightly sick. We went back to the car and headed for the
flat to wait. She'd have to walk all the way, we'd decided, for
fear of contaminating the cushions, and public transport was
out too.

It was only minutes later she was there, but it seemed
hours, and in fact her key was in the door and she was in the
bath, like an oversize mermaid, before I'd realized.

She was hot, tousled and very relieved. "I kissed him!" she
said. "I kissed him so hard he choked—I rubbed it all over him.
And I kissed both the guards. It *does* smell—ever so strong: like
cigar boxes. And I'm so glad that's over!"

I made a dash for her.

"Not yet!" she screamed and ducked her head. Fortunately
she heard me warn her to keep her eyes shut. Then Marcel put
away the stopwatch, pulled out the bathtub plug and we put
the shower on full. "Horrid," said Dulcinea, "like cheap lemon-
ade."

We both undressed her under the shower, and Marcel fetched her clothes, tactfully leaving me to wrap her in the towel, in case I'd got enough cocuficin to make me quarrel with him.

"Was I successful?" she said. "How'll we know? Can we go round and see?"

I told her I didn't expect that there would be anything to see. Marcel reckoned he might got booed; with any luck the effect would last until the vote, but he doubted that. The news would tell us if Untergang's popularity index had gone down, and how much. Marcel still wasn't bringing the clothes. I thought this was a mark of great delicacy, but instead he burst in without them as I was speaking. "We needn't wait! *Il est foutu!* Listen! You hear? I don't think there's going to *be* a vote!"

And certainly, apart from the ordinary noise of traffic, there was a row going on somewhere. We could hear yells, and a police tender going pah-*pah*, pah-*pah*, somewhere in the general direction of the conference. For the first time Dulcinea looked frightened.

"I hope you haven't made me do something stupid," she said.

"Steady, steady," I called after her—the two of them were hanging out of the window, Dulcinea half dressed—the wrong half—"it's probably a smash. Or a fire. Or the Algerians have chucked a bomb."

"I think," said Marcel, "they are having his head as a football." He'd stopped grinning.

After about ten minutes, during which the noise of battle got louder and nearer, an American helicopter went over low. From our flat we could see, as the agent had told us when we jibbed at the rent, up one of Haussmann's fine streets almost to the Étoile, designed to give a clear field of fire against approaching mobs, and that was precisely what was approaching at the moment. The helicopter did a circuit and came back, looking for something. Right at the limit of our field of vision, antlike figures appeared out of a general scampering pother that sounded like a rat hunt at Cruft's. The foremost ant appeared to be an Olympic runner. If so, his style wasn't very good. But he was covering ground remarkably fast in spite of that. I grabbed for our field glasses, but the helicopter, picking him out, spun round and landed between him and my line of vision; not, however, before I had recognized the athlete as Untergang: he was either in running kit or in vest and pants. Kicking feet were withdrawn into the cabin and the machine climbed out in a vast cloud of dust and wastepaper. The pursuers stood looking up at it, as beagles would if they'd treed a cat by mistake. Then they turned back in the direction of the mounting row which was coming from the other side of the Arc de Triomphe. Bricks and berets dotted the ground.

"Nom d'un nom de millions de mille bordels," said Marcel, and sat down on the floor. "Don't go and see what has happened. The police will break everybody's face."

From the din out of sight it was evident they were doing so already. Cocuficin had made its first appearance on the political scene, and already, so far as I was concerned, its last.

Face-breaking being in full swing, it took Chandra quite an hour to reach us with his report. The session had been abandoned all right. So far from enjoying the fun he'd had a frightful experience. He was shaking all over and as disturbed by what he had seen as I was when he told his story. Untergang had come in, smirking all round as usual—he'd posed with his arm round Fundament, sat down by him, and got out his papers. Then Fundament leaned over and said something which seemed to surprise him. Meanwhile the chairman was droning away. When he got to "I call on the first witness called by the United States, United Kingdom, and French governments jointly, Dr. Helmut Untergang" flashbulbs were going off all round. Up to that point nothing at all had happened. Then, as Untergang started, a steady change spread over all the faces round him. The Western boys had all been looking vacuous and the Eastern boys had been keeping up steady scowls (Untergang was really giving evidence on behalf of their tests too, and they knew it, but they still had to scowl). As the faces changed, Chandra said, "It was as if they all suddenly saw him as we have always seen him. Not anger to start with, disgust—it was as if a leper had started undressing among them and showing his ulcers, but there was no pity about it. The reaction of anger followed continuously. The disgust had reached me before it began, but soon I also could have killed him." Untergang wasn't particularly sensitive to atmosphere. He was too pleased with his brief to notice what his audience thought, but he happened to look up, and stopped short. He'd just said that we should be stout-hearted, and rather than risk the defeat of the Free World, free men everywhere would gladly face the termination of history; but this was not necessary—we had superior force on our side, and if, as his opponents suggested, some very small number of people must give up their lives through malignant disease to maintain that force, they were doing no more than every soldier was proud to do, and they should be honored by the Free World. Then he saw the face of the delegate opposite, who'd been applauding him wildly on behalf of the Formosa government, and looked down to see if he'd unwittingly wet his pants. The disgust on the man's face shook even Untergang. Possibly he wondered if he'd gone too far. Somebody said, "Mr. Chairman!" Then the Swiss delegate, who was a large, middle-aged neutral, got up from his place, walked steadily round to Untergang, and gave him a slap in the face that sounded like an antitank rifle. There was no stunned silence or anything, simply a colossal cheer, and they went for him in a body, from the chairman to the two police at the door. "It was a terrifying thing," said Chandra, "because I hated him as much myself at that moment. I wanted to castrate him—so I think, did they—and even with this insight I could not control myself from shouting."

Untergang himself had been pretty quick off the mark, I must say; he was helped by the fact that Dulcinea had also kissed his two bodyguards (that saved his life, I imagine, though it put both of them in hospital) and by the fact that within the next half minute the delegates had picked up enough releaser on themselves to start slugging one another. Chandra saw the chairman giving the Hungarian delegate a going-over with a ruler, and getting a knockout in exchange. Untergang got down the steps and dashed for his car, which was on the stand—but when he was half in the chauffeur spat in his face and slung him out again, so he'd had to run for it. Unfortunately he took his odor with him. Even the dogs had joined in.

"Where did the mob come from?" I asked.

"He must have picked it up on the way. But when I saw him there was no mob. Only the assembled diplomats of the world, acting like the wild hunt. This must never, never happen again. This stuff must be destroyed and never used. You have found the black face of the goddess—this is Untergang's own goddess, namely, Thanatos." Chandra was really upset—as pale as he could get without bleaching, and I didn't wonder at it, though it must have been a gratifying sight in its way. I made up my mind we ought to check if it was nonspecific—what Chandra said about dogs joining in was interesting: we heard after that a police stallion had had a go at him too, but its rider managed to stop it—evidently Man was less susceptible.

"It is a pity," said Marcel. "It set this basket of crabs fighting each other—so what? As for the general public, it only made them act as we all would like to act if we dared. It's a bottled Marseillaise. With it, we could turn the French imperialists out of Algeria, the American bases out of France, the Russians out of Hungary, and the bastards out of everywhere—we could motivate the public to resist. We could make them hate the people they ought to hate."

I told him not to be a bloody fool. It was one thing to let love loose in a bottle, quite another to let out hate, and what did he think the Cold War boys would do with the stuff if they got it? As for the bottled Marseillaise, it was great fun to say *"Tremblez, tyrans! et vous, perfides,"* but if he wanted Marat and Carrier he could keep them. All the same, it was our temptation in the wilderness. What was so depressing to me was that for years Untergang had been doing and saying things that should have stimulated disgust and hatred exactly like this in every sane human being, and saying them publicly on behalf of a democratic country—yet he still had office and a whole skin. Now he'd had a taste of being treated as the vermin he was, it had nothing to do with the leprosy he stood for—simply the fact that he'd been given an imperceptible smell which aroused unconscious territory-behavior. Tarunachandra, who by now was sitting there quoting the Gita, might be right, but the whole thing was pretty nasty and I wished we hadn't tried it. Dulcinea, as usual, was being reasonable—as if we two had put her up to it—and giving us *"Lift up your hearts."*

"Never again. Promise me. Let's stick to making them enjoy life, then they'll be bound to hate Dr. Untergang without going mad about it. Couldn't we get him to our classes? We might even make him enjoy life, after the fright he's had."

I doubted that, but didn't argue. We were all pretty subdued. Finally Marcel reminded us that it was time for a news bulletin, and we put it on in time to hear democratic indignation booming that Communists disguised as reporters had got in and attacked the delegates in an effort to break up the conference. Nothing ever caught Fundament off balance. And nothing untoward appeared in the papers. *Pravda*, when I managed to get it, said that the disguised *provocateurs* were fascists hired by the Americans.

There had in any case been so many dogfights at conferences of late that this one hardly stirred a ripple—as for the organizers, they postponed the session *sine die*, which meant until the protagonists were out of hospital and the generality of the delegates had lost the shiners they'd given each other. All of them were firmly convinced that outsiders started the trouble—added to that, by the time they'd each absorbed enough cocuficin into their own systems to be refractory to it and calm down, they were in prime condition to be mobbed by the crowd outside. Even their police escort had gone for them. "They feel as I did," said Chandra, "that somebody hit them first. Therefore somebody did hit them first. Probably they will repress the whole experience."

However, Marseillaise or no Marseillaise, we all agreed

that there should be no repetition; and this time Marcel associated himself with the opinion unreservedly. After one more experiment (which showed that cocuficin was in fact nonspecific for species and more active on stallions than Man), all reference to it was removed from the laboratory notes.

The final shock came three days after the Untergang operation, when Dulcinea had a very early miscarriage. This was worse for my morale and for my professional self-estimate as a student of fertility than it was for her health—in a sense it could even be called fortunate. But it wasn't until we heard that four of the typists (who'd watched in amazement the battle at the conference because, being women, they were emotionally unaffected by cocuficin) had also miscarried, and the coincidence was being talked about, that someone remembered Bruce's work. This showed that pregnancy and implantation in mice are seriously upset by the odor of a strange male, especially one of mature age. This was a new and quite unforeseen reason for letting cocuficin alone—for the present at least, though it had possibilities for the future. Toxicity apart from the behavioral effect hadn't occurred to us. All in all, we'd been pretty foolish. If Untergang had had a narrow escape, so had we.

We were still pretty shaken by the cocuficin debacle when we received a peculiar invitation; the possibility that the two might be connected gave us a good deal of anxiety. On the surface, the card which arrived was unexceptionable—it was delivered at the clinic, and it requested the pleasure of the company of Miss D. Fuentes y McGredy and of Dr. George Goggins at a small reception to meet the Rt. Reverend Dr. Stephen Gaudeamus. The trouble was that the reception was at a house belonging to the embassy, and the hostess was the wife of the First Secretary. Dulcinea was worried because they'd put us both on a single card. I was more concerned that Fundament might just possibly have a hand in it, and that he might have got wind that we were behind what had happened to his conference. But I told Dulcinea to look up Gaudeamus in *Who's Who,* and we sat down to consider him.

"It says," she read out, with her pretty forefinger in among the celebrities, "Gaudeamus, Stephen Athanasius, see Skegness, Bishop of. Skegness, Bishop of—since 1962, Rt. Rev. Stephen Athanasius Gaudeamus, D.D. b Oct 18 1918, s of late Prof. J. M. Gaudeamus FRS. M 1943, Alice Edwina Prosser, no c. Educ: Do you want it all?"

"Carry on," I said, "it might just possibly be important."

"Educ," Dulcinea continued, "Eton, New Coll. Oxford. Curate, St. John's, Stepney, 1941–44, All Saints, Belgravia 1944–46, Chaplain and Librarian, St. Radegund's College, 1946–48, Examining Chaplain to the Bishop of Metroland 1948–49, Personal Chaplain to the Deputy Earl Marshal, 1949–50, Hon. Canon of Clacton Cathedral 1949–57."

It had been a fairly steady and diverse climb via the Suffraganate of Windsor—the tailpiece was the most interesting part of it: "Hon. Chaplain and Vice-President, Marital Repairs Council. Recreations: sailing, bird ethology." Dulcinea shut the volume.

"I think," I said, "that it's probably quite all right. In fact this reception may be a very important engagement."

"But why a bishop?" said Dulcinea.

"Christian monogamy," I said, "remember? This is a reconnaissance flight."

"Then stay away—we don't want to be found out, do we?"

"I am not afraid," I said, "of being found out, as you call it. I have nothing up either sleeve. Nor have you, except what there should be there."

She was still doubtful. To check my own hunch, based on the shape of the bishop's growth-curve, I took the risk of dropping Boyo a note with the single question "Who is Gaudeamus?" The reply was equally succinct: "The next Archbish. Why do *you* want to know?"

The small size of the reception confirmed my impression. The others were makeweights to screen an inspection of myself and Dulcinea. Dr. Gaudeamus had not put in an appearance when we arrived, together—the horseshoe of faces was not exactly cordial, though it was trying hard, but before there could be an awkward silence we were seized, and my hand energetically shaken, by Horne Bros.

"I'm delighted that you could come, delighted, Dr. Goggins. Madam." He looked healthier than before—there wouldn't have been any chance now of overlooking the fact that he was a living organism, as I'd done at our first encounter. I asked him whether his wife was well, and the enthusiasm of his reply made it clear that even in ten minutes I'd been able to alter his life situation. I couldn't inquire, however, as Gaudeamus was shown in at that moment, led by an enormous pedigree Guernsey from the British Council, who smoked as if she were chewing the cud. Gaudeamus was a large, ruggery man with a gently rueful smile. He had a small, neat, violet-scented wife like a little sugar cake. Our introduction was quite cursory, the bishop went the rounds, and we were left, deliberately, talking to Horne Bros., who wouldn't let us move.

"You must brief me," I said to him. "I haven't very many direct ecclesiastical contacts."

"No?" said Horne Bros. "Oh, he's a rising churchman, very much a rising churchman; a very mature thinker, and personally, I hear, a very fine man."

"Well in with the people who. . . . form our national policies?" I asked him.

Horne Bros. nodded rapidly, reverently, and secretively— a large content for a single gesture-sequence, but it was all there. "Yes, yes, I believe great weight is attached to his judgment. And he's a personal friend. . . ."

The fade-out followed a signal given by the Guernsey. The other guests streamed off like schooling fish as she brought Dr. Gaudeamus and his wife into position; Horne Bros. smiled waxily at Dulcinea and retired immediately.

"Miss McGredy, Dr. Goggins," said the Guernsey, "I want you to meet Dr. and Mrs. Gaudeamus." *He* was being presented to *us*. I caught Gaudeamus's eye. It was a shrewd and extremely sensible eye, without a vestige of TDS about it. His courtesy to Dulcinea was genuine and spontaneous, but there was just that touch of calculation which showed me that he knew a good deal about us already. Dulcinea and the wife sidestepped, to avoid a lunge from the Guernsey, and I was on my own with him.

"I can see you've seen through me," said Gaudeamus. "As you've no doubt guessed, I'm here on reconnaissance. I'd rather have come and seen you privately, but I couldn't control the Embassy: I'm sorry about the transparent artifice."

"Not a bit," I said, "I've been poaching on your marriage guidance work."

"I understood you'd been cooperating in it," said Gaudeamus. "You preached a much better sermon to the press than they've ever had from me. In fact you almost exhausted the subject."

"That, I'm afraid, was the idea."

The episcopal eye was full of comprehension—it was also too knowledgeable for me to waste time flanneling it. "What I said wasn't entirely humbug," I told him. "It doesn't represent my own opinions, but when you want to help people you have to make some show of conforming with theirs, and if the press had made a song about what we were doing it would have put us out of business."

"Well," said Gaudeamus, "I certainly didn't come to complain. You seem to have helped a great many people. You've been the subject of debate on my committee—half of them wanted to fetch you to England to lecture to them (assuming, of course, that you'd be willing to do it)."

"And the other half . . . ?"

"Looked up your previous writings and thought you were a potentially dangerous influence. So I promised to talk to you personally and ask you questions."

"I'll answer them as frankly as I can."

"I'm sure you will. What I understand you're doing is to

draw on a large body of—traditional knowledge from other cultures to increase your pupils' physical satisfaction in marriage."

"Traditional," I said, "and scientific."

"Are you really preaching Christian matrimony to them as well?"

"Of course not. But from your point of view if they're happy they'll be more likely to stay married."

"Quite."

"And since, as you know, my collaborator and I are not married ourselves . . ."

"I knew that," said Gaudeamus, "and you'll notice it doesn't stop me from shaking hands with you. The point I've actually come to raise may strike you as quite academic—even incomprehensible. It's really, if you like, a problem of my own—it's concerned with the valuation you appear to put on pleasure."

The Guernsey had managed it very nicely; apart from Dulcinea and the little episcopal wife, who were in the opposite corner, we were in an empty room, and the Bishop let his voice become noticeably more resonant. It was his only concession to his office so far.

"What you're teaching these people to attain, I understand, is the keenest physical pleasure, in sensory terms, that you can."

"Yes. But that has effects on their other activities."

"I know. But I wonder whether that isn't possibly—from my own point of view, you understand—a false valuation of sexuality."

Pause for his point to be taken.

"I genuinely want to know. I'm concerned, as you will realize, to encourage people to make of their sexuality the use that God intended, if I can know what He intended. I can appreciate that you aren't. You probably don't view it teleologically, but you follow me?"

Formate on bird ethology, I thought. "I think I can actually answer the point," I said. "You could argue that the function of hearing isn't to enable us to enjoy Beethoven, but I can be more specific than that. Is it a Christian position that the pleasure is only there to guarantee reproduction?"

"It's one Christian position. I admit I incline to it. I'm not against pleasure in any sense, but pleasure rather easily becomes an end in itself."

"In man," I said, "either God or natural selection, we need not argue which, has made pleasure a much more important biological function of sexuality than reproduction, statistically at any rate."

"More important?"

"It's been more important statistically ever since one of our ancestors started mating all the year round and throughout pregnancy."

He thought hard about that.

"In fact, I can give you a figure. If we assume two matings a week, which is very low, and one nine-month pregnancy a year, the relative numerical importances of pleasure and reproduction are 103 to 1. I don't think that either God or natural selection altered the usual mammalian pattern to make 103 out of every 104 acts of intercourse functionless. In fact the real figure's probably more like 400 to 1. Now I suggest that a function of the pleasure generated by the excess is the maintenance of what I call pair-mating and you call Christian matrimony."

"I must have that again, if you don't mind."

He had it again. "Adult sexuality in man is predominantly a functional form of play. You may consider it as analogous to the pair-maintaining display of bowerbirds," I continued.

"I don't know bowerbirds, except from what I've read—but I know storks!" said Gaudeamus, kindling sincerely.

So starting from storks I sat down and opened to him the scriptures—Darwin, Freud, Lorenz in that order, going via the development of all-the-year-round mating and constant receptivity in primates to the division of human sexuality into infantile and adult halves, and bringing in gulls, geese, lyrebirds and finally, as the cherry on top, the human capacity for

Making an Aesthetic Value from a Physiological Original. It went down him like milk—there was no question of blinding him with science, because he knew a surprising amount of it already, but he'd never had it presented in that sequence at that speed. He filled up slowly with it from the feet to the ears like a plastic hot water bottle. At the end he was genuinely impressed. I could hear Dulcinea, who'd heard this lecture a few dozen times, shuffling and trying to maintain conversation with Mrs. Gaudeamus. I heard a penetrating whisper once, "Stephen's being outpreached!" All the time I was talking my eye was on a mental slip, passed to me from the usual source, which said "M. 1943, Alice Edwina Prosser, no c."

"Well, it is said," said Gaudeamus, coming out of a kind of reverie, "that nobody was ever convinced by argument. I wouldn't yet be certain you've convinced me, but you've certainly cleared my mind. I only wish I could ask you for that . . . address . . . in writing in case by tomorrow I feel you've overpersuaded me by sheer density of thought. . . ." He smiled like a well-filled baby letting go of the nipple.

"Here you are," I said and handed him a reprint of the same lecture. He took it and pocketed it.

"And exhortation is supposed to be my profession," said Gaudeamus. "I know a virtuoso performance when I see one. You weren't ever by any chance a Jesuit?"

"I apologize," I said, "for lecturing."

Dulcinea's little chuckle didn't spoil the atmosphere, but I noticed that Gaudeamus wasn't quite at ease, and wondered. That little paper slip kept being put in front of me.

"Well, now you've got to take the consequences," said Gaudeamus, gathering himself together for an effort. "You may wish you hadn't converted me." He looked over his shoulder at Alice Edwina and Dulcinea. "Come and join us, my dear. We'll do this jointly. Dr. Goggins, I've always felt, and I know my wife has always felt, that from her point of view our own married life is not all it could be." Alice Edwina née Prosser moved up in support, looking tense, but hopeful.

"Of course," I said, "we'll be delighted to help. In any way we can."

During the summer, chiefly at Dulcinea's insistence, we shut down the courses for a month and went down to La Napoule. Dulcinea rebrowned herself in sections—needlessly, I thought, because her color is naturally Renoir not Rubens, even in winter—but it gave me time to catch up on some of my own fieldwork for the first time since I left India. The classes had shown up a nasty gap in it, because the thousands of feet of film we'd taken in the past and scored for somatotype were all shot in non-European cultures, and I had nothing European at all, either for research purposes or as background for the classes. This meant, of course, that we had only verbal evidence of the behavior range we were trying to modify. Accordingly I found the private lido where most of the Free World went on Saturdays. While Dulcinea lay on the beach, I set up a hide and managed to get a few hundred feet at close quarters and a lot more telephoto, most of it in color, in case we ever got enough to score hair color as well as body build. This wasn't enough to analyze, but it was enough to give some idea what the range of behavior had been before we started to interfere with it.

We got the usual crop of biases in the material. American pairs were much less wary than Nato-English: as with the gorillas I'd filmed when I was doing my thesis, it was the early stages of mating which were hardest to get, before the attention of the pairs became fully absorbed; after that it was usually easy—these Free World pairs weren't quite as easily disturbed as the gorillas, but, of course, likely to be far more aggressive. The only other animal which regularly attacks observers on sight is, so far as I know, the tawny owl. Dulcinea was frightened for my personal safety when she found out what I was doing and threatened to come with me.

That very day, as it happened, the hide collapsed. The male I was filming got his trunks more or less on and came cantering up (he'd kept his spectacles on his nose throughout, I noticed—even in his previous condition he'd been twin brother to Horne Bros., only waiting for the window dressers to deal with him).

"I say," he puffed, "what the devil do you think you're doing?"

I'd realized, of course, that we might have an emergency of this kind.

"Sshhh!" I said, pointing into some unlikely looking grass—"Reed pipit!"

"Reed pipit my Aunt Fanny! You bloody little blackmailer!"

I was ready for him. "Here, I say!" I shouted, flinging down the rest of the hide, and taking care not to give him time to say anything more, "you've ruined ten years' work. An egg, oh God! an egg!—something nobody ever filmed before. And you stick your fat head in the light. That bird will desert. It's gone. It won't come back! Couldn't you see I was filming? Well, couldn't you? What the devil do you mean by creeping up like that? I've a good mind to break your neck!"

"Yes, but . . ." he started; I knew it was all right when I saw him wavering in the face of a threat display.

His inamorata, who'd turned over on her tummy and lain there trying to be invisible, had recovered, and rolled rapidly into a clump of marram, fielding her two-piece on the way; she was now frantically signaling to him to desist.

"But nothing," I said. "I think you owe me an apology, old chap. I'm sorry, for my part, if I swore at you. You weren't to know. But it's a bit disappointing, you know. What did you want, anyhow?"

"Oh—ah . . . huh!"

He shambled off. After that Dulcinea carried out her threat and came with me whenever she saw me with the camera. In point of fact, however, this proved the ideal solution, because the one object mating pairs invariably seemed to ignore was another mating pair—Dulcinea herself was therefore the ideal hide. All the rest of my material was shot over her shoulder, using her hair as cover for the smaller camera, and the results were first rate. I wondered why I'd never thought of it before.

We did, in fact, eventually solve the problem of photography under controlled indoor conditions, by getting the class entrants to spend a couple of nights in the institute. We had already asked them to take their body temperatures for one full ovarian cycle, and by finding a pretext for making them take a two A.M. reading we could usually induce them to come in and be woken dead on time by telephone. The building being air-conditioned with unopenable windows we only needed introduce a little deoxy-3-blindmycin into the air intake, and then run up the temperature to get rid of the bedclothes, for photographic conditions to be ideal. In fact, if this got hot enough, we could photograph our pairs by the infrared they radiated themselves. The camera and image converter were housed in the wardrobe and started by a seismo-switch from the bed, which made the recording procedure fully automatic. The pictures used later in the textbook which we did for sixth forms and in the recent schools transmissions on television were all taken on this setup; it also enabled us to follow our pupils throughout several stages of proficiency without embarrassing them.

By the late autumn we finally felt ready to risk the synthesis of 3-blindmycin itself, with full precautions. Unlike the others, which were oils, it was a pinkish solid crystallizing in long prisms. The scent was very like that of the deoxy-compound, but very much stronger, and it was certainly far more active—how much more it was not possible to judge without human trials. Apart from the familiar effects, there was a progressive flush with it which went up into your hair roots and made your ears thump. It also increased the daytime activity of mice, even in fantastically small amounts—about three molecules per mouse —and we used this as a sensitive means of assay.

The easiest way of handling it was in the absorbed state— we began absorbing it on lard, which is the conventional medium for holding flower perfumes, but there were difficulties in feeding this to the animals, and if we mixed it with food pellets the lard contaminated the hoppers and got on the coats of the mice. Finally Marcel had the idea of absorbing it on cheese, exposed to the vapor in centimeter-thick slices, exactly as he'd done with soap. This could be cut up without waste, but better still, we found it no longer affected Man on contact, owing to the acid conditions at the surface of the slice, which kept the vapor inside. This meant that practically no 3-blind-mycin got into the air—we were able to use the ordinary animal house, with normal ventilation, and the amount appearing in the animals' breath, though it was sufficient to affect mice in the other end of a double cage, wasn't enough to affect the girls who looked after them. They were warned against tasting the cheese—we thought of dyeing it, but didn't—we made them handle it with forceps and masks and kept a close watch on the pregnancy and resignation rate, but there were no big swings. What we wanted now, of course, was a critical human experiment, but I put my foot down about using it at the clinic until all the test-tube work had been completed.

All this, of course, took time. For the first time I began to feel the strain. In fact, it very soon became clear that with our other preoccupations and the exponential growth of the classes we should have to divide them and engage instructors. We were making more and more use of recordings, but this only increased our handling power and the size of the courses, and in the later stages personal instruction was quite essential. This gave me a great deal of anxiety. The whole success of the project had depended on keeping the thing in our own hands—instructors would have to be let into a good deal which required tact, including the use of fortified soap, and I mistrusted the possible result. I myself was willing to carry on—it was Dulcinea who was having the worst of it, and, more serious from the point of view of our private life, she was becoming a little bored with the whole subject of mating. I had been afraid of this, because unlike me she hadn't really the research motivation. She was being asked, after all, to make a business, a hobby, and a relaxation out of the same thing. It was only her preoccupation with marital happiness that kept her going.

I was obliged to agree in the end to her choosing herself a couple of assistants. I was against appointing them from the classes—I felt we should choose suitable people first and then train them. Dulcinea could do this admirably from her side, and she started very tentatively to interview possibles. We invited Marcel's Minouche, but she was already too busy. As they were going to treat my patients, or people who stood in a professional relationship to me, I felt, moreover, that on ethical grounds I would have to examine the candidates practically myself. Dulcinea, who is reasonableness itself and has never been jealous, fully appreciated this when I made it clear and was quite willing. "You examine them," she said, "and I'll examine the man, when we find one." I didn't like to feel, however, that she would be exposed to any unpleasantness when it came to picking male instructors, because I knew she would make no fuss if she found the job distasteful, and she isn't naturally promiscuous.

The difficulty, however, never arose, because two people whose proficiency I already accepted became available. Better still, they were husband and wife—the ideal arrangement. Out of the blue, they arrived at the laboratory and actually asked for a job. I arrived and found them sitting in my armchairs and smoking my cigarettes.

They were, as a matter of fact, of Arab origin—or rather Ahmed was, while his wife was half-Arab, half-Maltese. Ahmed had been at Trinity. Later I'd taught him physiology. What was more, I had personal knowledge of their suitability.

On my second furlough in England, the year before I came to Paris, I'd had an urgent postal request from Boyo, sent me care of the Royal Society of Medicine, to consult with a Middle Eastern client of his on my way to India. The client turned out to be the King of Asphaltum. Normally I would have refused this assignment on ethical grounds—Chibouk et-Twatt was and is a thoroughly nasty piece of work. Before he fell foul of the oil companies and was deposed, he lived in the style of Caligula, in a million-pound palace designed by Corbusier on a patch of desert containing the oil refinery, the rocket base, half a million impoverished subjects, and the town, which was all new and full of oilmen, spies, and the Free World generally living it up to the limit. He operated a slave trade which was written into the lease of the rocket base and therefore sacrosanct, even when his subordinates bagged an unusually good-looking tourist—the caravans still got Free World escort.

I agreed to go, eventually, on grounds of professional experience. I knew Chibouk had a large library of untranslated Arabic texts on my subject. His own knowledge of it was also said to be considerable (he'd had enough practice), and some of his subordinates knew more still.

Chibouk had arranged to send his emissary with a royal plane to meet me at Aden, and I was told that the emissary would be his *wazir el-haram,* or Minister of Reproductive Supply; what I hadn't expected was that I'd be met by one of my former physiology students, namely Ahmed, in European clothes and wearing his Trinity tie. He had taken his new job straight from graduation—Chibouk wanted a man who wouldn't be at a disadvantage in dealing with the Free World. He was delighted to see me. In fact, probably the most valuable part of my visit was the information he gave me on the plane flying over the Aden desert. He was naturally cagey about the king's personal affairs. When I asked about the monarch, he drew his finger round his neck from front to back about an inch above his Trinity tie, put out his tongue, and made his eyes bulge to indicate strangulation. To change the subject I asked him if he wasn't still physically overequipped for his job, by traditional standards.

"I am," he said, "but I am fortunate. The expense of an Aga is now too great, and they displease the Orthodox faithful. We find today that in an officer of integrity such as myself personal experience is an advantage."

The visit in the main was disappointing, however. I was housed not in the palace but in a Greek hotel. Each morning I was driven in with an escort of four irregular cavalry through the sentries, round the nonrepresentational fountain, and into the reception suite Chibouk kept for Europeans, and used for the oilmen and the Free World, which was equipped with Chippendale chairs.

Chibouk couldn't sit in any of these, even in European dress. The reason for my visit was evident at a glance, and he wasted no time. Ahmed interpreted.

"His Majesty has just said, 'My belly. It now limits my performance.'"

I wasn't surprised to hear it and suggested that we might manage to bring it under control by dieting.

"His Majesty has just said, 'Impossible. All the American doctors want to do that. I sent for you to tell me how to circumvent it. My wives are being injured.'"

This was a straight enough problem in somatotypology, which I'd dealt with before, and Chibouk, to make things easier, was reported to have the best collection in the world. With his consent I made Ahmed parade a sample of those who were under five feet in height, picked the most intelligent, and arranged for them to instruct the others. After a few days' practice under my direction, the problem was solved. Chibouk was as pleased as Punch, and the women, so far as one could judge, were very relieved.

I was sent for, on the morning after we'd finished, with a double cavalry escort, to receive a long speech of thanks, a gold box of medium quality containing £50 in sovereigns, and a large collection of miscellanea, from golf clubs to cocktail cabinets; they were all of very good workmanship but I noticed they were all things Chibouk didn't use. From a plaque inside one traveling case which said it was a token of personal esteem from his Britannic Majesty to H.S.H. Chibouk et-Twatt, K.G., etc., I guessed where the old skinflint had got them. I was never given a chance to ask him for research facilities—

I noticed that he was very keen to stress it was my last day among them and my plane had been ordered for next morning. At ten the British arrived. A banquet ran from eleven to four and dovetailed with a display of cavalry riding from four to six, a hummum bath from six until nine, after which we drove to a nightclub.

I was getting increasingly anxious to be on my way. The British Consul was interpreting, Ahmed having faded out, and everything had to be shouted against the band, which was going full blast. Chibouk drank buckets of sherbet. I had avoided all reference to my work, but he seemed keen now to draw me.

"He says he never finds our thin women attractive," said the consul, a dry little officer who was doing his duty, hating it, and obviously blaming me. There happened to be a strikingly pretty, willowy, half-Maltese girl sitting with some oilmen, who'd been teaching her to jive. I asked Chibouk if he didn't find her nice.

"He asks if she is the European ideal?"

"Well, she's not bad by any standards."

"He asks if she is your ideal," said the consul; then, without batting an eyelid, "I know this bloke—do be a bit careful."

I asked him if he could translate a Charles Boyer shrug. He tried, but it took a great deal of Arabic.

Ten minutes later, when I'd forgotten all this, the lights suddenly went out. This had happened several times while I'd been at the hotel—the supply was overloaded by all the new neon signs in town. There was a certain amount of commotion, but we sat still, and presently they came on again. It was some time later that I noticed the Maltese girl was gone, and the oilmen were holding an indignation meeting. After a bit I heard them being chucked out—rather roughly, I thought.

I was dead tired when I escaped from Chibouk's gratitude, by which time it was two o'clock. I undressed as soon as I got to my room and was just about to find the shower when I noticed something going on under the mosquito curtains round my bed. I picked up one of His Britannic Majesty's presentation golf clubs and went to investigate. It was the Maltese lady: she was neatly packed up with silk rope, arranged so that it kept her quiet without spoiling her line. There was a small pillow under her middle, and she was chewing on a rubber ball, kept in place by one of her own stockings. The rest of her clothes had been neatly folded and were lying alongside. Round her middle was a large red-white-and-blue bow, which might have come off a Coronation easter egg, holding a gold embossed card with Chibouk's arms and the handwritten words WITH COMPLIMENTS.

I put down the golf club and started to undo this Andromeda as fast as I could, wondering which was the best language for an apology. While I untied her hands, she seemed to be waiting for me to declare my intentions; when I removed the rubber ball, however, she'd decided they were honorable, and she settled the linguistic problem by belting me across the face as hard as she could and screaming in Italian, "Vermin! Eunuch! Carrion! First you have me stolen—then you don't want me!"

Fortunately, she hit me three times in quick succession before starting with her nails—I was distinctly vulnerable—and the three smacks must have sounded like the conventional call for an Oriental servant, because two characters in kaftans bounded out of the bathroom and between us we set about restoring the status quo. One of them was Ahmed.

"It is written, leave well alone, Excellency," he said, catching her hands with the skill of evident practice, "she was well as she was."

"I'd have thought you at least would have known better than this," I told him. "Undo her at once, blast you! Chibouk may think this is a great joke, but rape isn't my idea of one." I retrieved my pants.

"You heard, Excellency, what she said," said Ahmed, turning her over to fix her elbows.

"And you heard what I said. You didn't learn this lot at

Cambridge. Go on: *imshi*—and take her with you. The poor girl will be disgraced."

"She is disgraced when you expressed public interest in her," said Ahmed, checking over the job. "If you send her home a virgin she is also ridiculous." He put back her cushion.

"You've entertained too many Free World sales representatives," I said, firmly. "I'm not raping any women. You underrate my moral standards."

"You want her to go home and look very silly? Why did you then say you like her?"

I was adamant.

"Then, Excellency, she must be disposed of, so her relatives do not make trouble. You send her back, they'll think you find she is no good. This is most unjust to her."

I was beginning to have the uncomfortable feeling that the Maltese lady's contortions were being timed to support what Ahmed was saying. Evidently she understood English.

"Are you telling me she wants to be ravished?"

"It would be unjust to her otherwise."

"Look, my dear," I said to Andromeda, "do you understand? Do you really mean you want me to—be intimate with you?" She nodded vigorously.

"Then take that thing out of her mouth and undo her," I said to Ahmed. "If she's willing, we needn't treat her like that—anyone would think we were drenching a horse."

I started on the stocking. Ahmed snatched my hand away.

"No Excellency, no—she must not consent, or she is disgraced. You must ravish her. She for her part must resist—it is written. I warn you, she is strong, it would be too difficult, also very noisy, and you are unpracticed."

"And if I don't, she's equally disgraced?"

"No, worse."

"Well, what happens to her afterward? Is she my property, or what?"

"She has been given to a guest of Chibouk—she can marry anyone she chooses, *inshallah*—anyone. But if you refuse her, a beggar only."

It was a peculiar arrangement. Evidently, however, Allah had willed her to marry Ahmed. Here they both were in my laboratory.

Ahmed's wife—her name was Marousia—was quite free from embarrassment at meeting me again. She'd come on a great deal since then through living with Ahmed—he, by contrast, was rather less boisterous, now he was out of his own culture, and he badly needed my help. Chibouk had invited a Russian trade delegation and shut the rocket base—a week later his nephew was popped over the border from somewhere with unlimited cash and arms, so Chibouk was now living in reduced circumstances in Geneva, his effects had been sold up, his collection divided among the Medes and Persians, and Ahmed had had to run for his life. I didn't like to worry Dulcinea with the whole story, but we met the Ahmeds, took them out to dinner a few times, and were both of us satisfied that under supervision they were not too far culturally from our class members to be reliable instructors; Ahmed himself showed a grasp of the delicacy of our relations with the Church, for example, which made me quite confident that we could trust him not to be tactless. I didn't feel, though his English was perfect, that he should give the actual lectures, as he'd mixed a lot with oilmen, and was a little inclined to misweigh his words when describing sexual behavior. Accordingly, my own commentaries were tape-recorded for Ahmed's half of the class. Dulcinea took Marousia under her wing, and after a few weeks they could have been old schoolmates, or sisters. In fact, Dulcinea was laughing more, I noticed, than at any time since the Otto episode. On one or two occasions when Ahmed was tiresome, Marousia dealt with him by making muffled noises as if she'd got something in her mouth, which sent Dulcinea into fits and shut Ahmed up on the spot. All risks being weighed, I thought they were a valuable acquisition; moreover, they were back in the clear with the Free World, because Chibouk's nephew had sold the oil wells to the Chinese as soon as he was well settled, and the old regime was back in favor. Unfortunately for Chibouk, he'd also got a substantial Chinese garrison in before announcing the change of ownership; this meant Ahmed's services wouldn't probably be required in Asphaltum for a long time.

There was one important legacy of the past still brewing. There was Otto. We didn't talk about him, but when Dulcinea got unusually quiet I knew what she had in her mind. This had been less regularly periodic recently, but of course it had to come, and it came. One morning I went into the laboratory and found Otto sitting there. He was eating sandwiches out of a napkin, and "excuse-excuse" kept on steadily through the whole process. He didn't get up, or stop eating when I came in. And I was completely flummoxed what to say to him. What does one say to open the conversation with a man whose wife one has stolen, even if she was only a wife pro tem and the marriage was a bent one? On past occasions I'd never had to decide, because the aggrieved party had always started the ball rolling, or rather, he'd thrown it at my head. Otto couldn't because his mouth was full. But even when he'd taken a big swallow and wiped off his mouth on his sleeve, his eyes didn't look like physical violence, and I still hadn't grasped the initiative.

Otto said, "So we mate again."

"Who do?"

"We do. After two years again. You doing nicely?"

"Very nicely," I said, wondering if I ought to apologize and explain that after all it was better thus—the trouble was that it sounded like *"Because,"* or *"Until,"* and I just couldn't make the script convincing.

"You cure her headaches? Better than aspirin. I rub her neck does not do it—so where you rub her, eh?" He began to erupt sandwich crumbs over himself. The noise was more like backfiring than laughter, but at least he obviously wasn't going to be heavy about it.

"You ask you, what I want?"

"Well, I hadn't—I was actually going to ask *you*," I said, "but I don't mind waiting till you've finished your breakfast. Shall I get them to make you a cup of coffee?"

He held up a dirty forefinger with a knobby ring on it. "No, thank you. Poison."

"Well, be reasonable," I said, "if I meant to poison you I wouldn't do it with anything you can put in coffee."

"No, no, not you—is coffee is poison. Is why your color is very unhealthy. Shall I tell you something? Is caffeine make your life very very short."

"Robertson kept mice throughout life with nothing to drink but black coffee," I said, "and they lived just as long as controls."

"Is animal experiment, no good, only makes science confused. Why you waste time on animals, eh?"

"I don't, except when the stuff would be too dangerous to try in man," I said. "Man is my concern."

"Thought it was woman," said Otto.

I ignored him. "And I'm very glad you came in—I've been wanting to see you to get you to sign something for us."

"To sign?" The color started to go out of his face at the idea of signing anything. I hadn't meant to frighten him, but I had, and this was quite a good start. "Why should I sign anything?" he said, looking shaky.

"Just an affidavit."

"You try to catch me out. I know I must not sign. If I practice, all right—nobody, not the President, he cannot stop me—but if I sign something, finish. You think you're mighty clever but this I know I must not sign."

"Listen, I don't want you to sign a prescription . . ."

"Not bloody likely I sign a prescription. You are tricky. No more I sign a certificate."

"I don't want you to pose as a registered doctor and I'm not trying to catch you," I said.

"No, I should hope not! You qualified doctors, all alike, all in conspiring for me."

"Only to give us a written statement that you aren't Dulcinea's husband."

"Not with perjury neither," said Otto. "I am her husband."

"Can you produce a marriage certificate?"

"Is in Hungary." He took another sandwich out of the

napkin and bit it like a leaf-cutting bee. "Can you produce a not-marriaged certificate?" he said with his mouth full.

"Dulcinea says you were never really married to her, that you've got another wife living, and that the whole thing was a fake."

"She says, she says," said Otto. "Too true I was married already, but this marriage was no good; my first wife was not finished—she was too little, understand?—and we both tell too many lies. Was phony. This marriage, now, was all right. Sure I am her husband; why you want this certificate anyhow? After all, you got her, haven't you?"

"We want to get married."

"You want, but to my wife you can't—don't blame me: I didn't make this. If it was me, we all have all the wives we like, but God upset all that. And the government. Don't blame me."

"I don't believe she is your wife. She says she isn't."

"Well, I should know, shouldn't I? You think she's right, why don't you go ahead? You got her now not married, come to think of it, why you bother anyway?"

He emptied his mouth.

"You should learn, don't believe women. When they want to be respectable they say any damn thing."

"I still want your signature," I said.

"And I still say not bloody doing."

"Right," I said. "That settles that. Now, what can I do for you?"

"You can't do nothing. What you mean you can do for me?"

"You called to see me, remember?"

He put the entire sandwich in. It didn't fit, so he pushed with his thumbs.

"Wah?"

"You didn't come here to eat your lunch. What did you want?"

"Oh, that. A job."

"Doing what?"

"In your clinic. I hear about your clinic—very good idea, why didn't I think of it, my wife doing beautifully."

"You think you'd do beautifully too?"

"After all, think—I teach her."

"You forget," I said, "the instruction is practical." (How the dickens has he found out about it? This will ruin everything.) "Aren't you a bit past that kind of thing?"

He grinned all over his face, crumbs and all. "Not at all—no coffee! When I am a hundred I shall still be working. Whereas no doubt you will be drooping. You doctors think you know damn all, but you know damn nothing—this I will teach. You give me the old ones—if they have not drink too much coffee and be vaccinated (vaccinated is another bad thing, makes the virility very flabby), I shall rub their necks, and their wives will frighten! Am I begin tomorrow?"

"No, you won't."

He shrugged his shoulders. "You ask her, then—she'll tell you, she has felt me."

"I have," I said, "and she has told me." He looked a bit abashed. "By all accounts you weren't outstanding."

"She would not concentrate." He shook his head slowly, shedding crumbs all the time. They seemed to come out of his nose like cinders out of a locomotive.

"Well," I said, "I'm sorry I can't oblige you."

"They have babies ever?" said Otto.

"And we don't require the services of an abortionist."

"I am not," said Otto, "an abortionist. Not down below or skippings or pills or anything illegal. I make them finish by rubbing the neck—you tell me where is a law you mustn't make them finish by rubbing the neck. My conscience is all right. I am unblackmailable." He shook out the napkin full of crumbs all over the place. "Whereas you pinch people's wives to teach —how was it?—top bishops about Christian marrying, very good! I am surprised at you."

The interview was awkward and in the end pretty unconclusive. Otto shuffled off. He seemed unfortunately well informed. He didn't actually demand money or utter threats.

He simply hung around. When he left he said he'd be back. I sent a message to Marcel, who was at the library, to join me at the flat and went back before Otto could get there to upset Dulcinea.

As it was, he didn't try. Dulcinea took it quietly, too quietly; she'd been expecting it. Marcel was brisk to the point of exasperation.

"Well, there must be something in his past life we can get him on—go on, *chérie*, think; he's such a crook it ought to be easy."

"Shut up," said Dulcinea. "It won't be easy. I know him. I don't want to hurt him, either, and I don't want him to hurt us. You couldn't take him on—for a little while? I expect he's had a bad season."

I explained to her that we couldn't possibly, even out of pity. Of course, she knew that as well as I did. Otto among the Smiths would finish us all—besides, it would be covering unqualified practice.

"We must make him fall hard down stairs, then," said Marcel.

"Don't be a bloody fool. We wait until we see how much he wants. He hasn't asked for anything."

We both slept badly, and Dulcinea talked a lot in her sleep, which she'd never done before. Next day Otto was back, hanging about the lab. He obviously knew his onions. He wasn't going to ask for anything, for fear I'd got witnesses or a tape ready for him. He was just going to be in and out until I bid. He fell in alongside when I went to lunch, but I didn't invite him as he hoped. When I got back, he was there in my room again with sandwiches and a bottle of ketchup; there was ketchup on my carpet and a ketchup ring on my desk. My clinic session that day was an evening affair. I made up my mind to tell Otto that if he even tried to come to the clinic, I'd do him a mischief. When I got ready to go, I found him copying the telephone number and the address of the flat out of my desk book. Before I could say what I was going to say, about staying away from the clinic, and adding "from

Dulcinea," if he wanted a whole skin, he gave me a sweet smile. "Tonight," he said, "I go to a show. Girls." And he went out.

Otto was certainly a master of psychological warfare. I telephoned to warn Dulcinea he might be coming, but when I got back from the clinic he hadn't appeared. Evidently he had gone to the show as he said.

The telephone rang as we were undressing. Dulcinea jumped violently. "This is it," she said. She was naked, and she seemed to have shrunk with worry. She shivered a little as I went to take the call.

I couldn't believe my ears. I was a long time getting the message straight, and Dulcinea came beside me, her arms round herself. "What does he want?"

I hung up. "That was the hospital," I told her. "Otto has been taken ill. He's in the psychiatric unit."

Her arms dropped. "What do you mean, ill?"

"Well, he's in a padded cell."

"Why?"

I must have sounded indecently relieved. "It looks as if that's that," I said. "He appears to have gone berserk. He was brought in by the police. All I know is that he went to a show at the Mayol and started assaulting the girls. The hospital reports that he's violent. Beyond that I've no information. And I've been called to examine him. *In manus nostras, Domine.* Anyhow, it's convenient."

To my surprise, Dulcinea flew at me.

"You and Marcel did this, didn't you?"

"Certainly not—how could we have done?"

"What a dirty trick! And you promised me, after what you did to Untergang!"

"I assure you on my honor that we had nothing to do with it."

"And I said once that you weren't a swine!"

"Look," I said, "have you ever known me to tell you a lie?"

"No," said Dulcinea, "but I've heard you dealing with

other people. And I knew Otto—I lived with him for eighteen months—are you suggesting that he just went and did this?"

"I never said he hasn't had some 3-blindmycin," I said; "in fact it sounds as if he's had a lot of it. But we didn't give it to him. Knowing his habits, my preliminary guess is that he got into the animal house and pinched some treated cheese."

"Which you put where you knew he'd have to pass it."

"Certainly not."

"Are you sure?" she said.

"I wish you'd believe me—really."

"I suppose I shall have to. Are you sure Marcel didn't?"

"I doubt it. If he did I'll break his neck." The idea had crossed my mind, about Marcel, but I hoped he had more sense. "But he can't have done. He wasn't in the lab today."

"The whole thing's beastly." Her face was screwing up dangerously.

I thought it was nice of her to cry for Otto. It meant that she had never accepted him without some affection.

"Don't cry," I said, "please. Any trouble he's in I'll get him out of. Are you satisfied?"

"Yes," she said. "I suppose I shall have to be. What are you going to do with him?"

"I'll go and see what he's like now. Ring up Marcel, get him out of bed if necessary, and tell him what's happened."

Otto was sitting on the floor in the pad. They'd taken his suspenders, shoes, and tie, and both he and the male nurse on duty showed signs of struggle. There was a policeman standing in the duty room. He saluted sharply. It looked as if someone had lately clobbered him, too. Otto was caressing, with profound affection, the bulges in the rubber cushions. For the moment he seemed quite happy.

"Leave him alone while he's quiet," I said. "What happened?"

Apparently he'd left us shortly before eight and gone straight to the theatre, as he said he would. The *ouvreuse* who tried to sell him some postcards saw him settle down, produce a packet and a bottle of yoghurt, complete with a plastic spoon, and wait for the show. At that time he appeared normal. Nothing had happened until the last parade before the interval, when the girls had come down the promenade in the middle of the stalls, in the nude, for the start of the closing number. The leading girl was one I knew—her name was Mado, and I'd considered her as a possible assistant instructress for the classes if we ever needed one. As she passed Otto, he'd got over the rail onto the promenade and started removing her *minimum*. She'd been too amazed to shout at first, and the public took it for a gag, but as the thing was stuck on with gum arabic in accordance with police regulations he hurt something more than her dignity. Mado belted him with a shoe, the other girls had joined in, the lights went up, and Otto was handed over to the police. As he'd then made love to them too, *faute de mieux,* in spite of being beaten up all the way from the Mayol to the clink, they'd sent him on to the hospital, and here he was.

When Marcel arrived we reviewed the facts carefully. He swore himself black that he'd had no hand in it, and knowing he hadn't been in, I believed him. There was no doubt whatever in our minds that Otto must have had some of our cheese. A count in the animal-house store showed that there were two slices missing. On inquiry, we found that some of this and the empty yoghurt bottle had been recovered when he was arrested, and we had them sent round for examination.

"But it must have taken a devil of a time to act," said Marcel. "What did he do with it? Chew it slowly?"

"We don't know exactly when he got to the cheese," I said, "but it's critically important. This is your human experiment, boy. Are you quite sure . . . ?"

"Look, we've had that all out. I wasn't in the lab. Ask the gateman." I had, and he wasn't.

"The joke is that it's dramatic irony with a vengeance—" I went on, "Otto doesn't approve of animal experiments; they confuse science. He was urging me to stick to human subjects. And he doesn't approve of coffee, or he'd probably have had his supper like a Christian in a café instead of mixing it with sex."

They rang to tell us the sample was on its way up. When it came, it was undoubtedly our cheese, so that settled that. We decided that the reason it hadn't acted earlier was that Otto had put half a pint of yoghurt on top of it. So long as there was plenty of lactic acid about, nothing had happened, but he kept on eating the cheese, and the dose was cumulative: once the lactate started to run out, he had got the lot.

After that we weighed the remaining cheese. We found by subtraction that he'd eaten 75 grams at 1 microgram 3-blindmycin per kilo, so the maximum dose he could have had was 0.075 microgram. Probably he had shown a response equivalent to much less—say 0.05 microgram. This wasn't only more than enough—it had sent him completely up the wall for twelve hours. From the animal studies, that made the effective dose for Otto, who was heavy, about 0.001 microgram. Now the vial in our fridge, which we hadn't yet opened, contained, we knew, at least one gram and possibly two. By a simple sum, that meant that we had enough there to physic $\frac{1,000 \times 1,000}{0.001} = 1,000,000,000$ people the same size as Otto.

I think that that night my appreciation of figures was still blunted by relief that I could now deal with Otto from a position of strength. Actually this estimate was an exaggeration—it was two orders of magnitude too big, since for reasons I needn't recount there is a dogleg in the response curve at about 0.02 microgram. Accordingly, the answer was really more like 10,000,000. But even that would have been, to put it mildly, impressive. We assayed the remaining cheese to see that it hadn't by some accident become overloaded, but there was no mistake. The dose which had floored Otto was about the amount of sugar he'd get if we'd dissolved a lump in a swimming bath and given him a spoonful.

By this time it was eight o'clock in the morning, zero plus twelve. When I looked in through the spyhole in the pad, Otto was still sitting on the floor, but he'd stopped patting the bulges in the padding. Instead, he was examining his stockinged feet with an air of really pitiful dejection. "Excuse-excuse," had changed in pitch to "cheese-cheese."

"He's quite quiet," said the male nurse, "but he's been muttering like that about cheese. Do you want any help, sir?"

I sent him away and went into put Otto out of his misery.

He neither greeted me nor expostulated. "It was the cheese?" he said, as soon as I was in.

I nodded.

"You did this."

I pointed out that as he must have opened two doors marked "Keep out," a wire screen marked "DANGER," a refrigerator, and a zinc box in order to find any cheese, he couldn't maintain that hypothesis.

Otto wasn't logical yet, however. "You mean me to find it," he said, sadly. "You know I like cheese. You have pinched my wife, now you send me crazy. You are a little bastard— I get even with you."

I sat down on the floor and explained to him that he wasn't being quite fair to either of us and evidently didn't appreciate his position. He'd got himself into this trouble by his own unaided efforts. If he liked he could get himself out in the same way. I would have preferred to help him, however, since he had been an acquaintance of Dulcinea's, and if he liked I would certify him. That would stop any more police unpleasantness, and he could be cured and discharged after a suitable interval. Alternatively, if that was what he wanted, I'd testify that he was sane. In that case he would get several years for being a dirty old man.

Otto looked at me as if I were a hatful of snakes.

However, I said, if he saw reason and stopped calling me names, he could be suffering from a combination of any unethically promoted drug he cared to name with alcohol, and his lapse was due to synergism.

"Is what?"

"Mixing your drinks."

"But I don't drink—I disapprove."

"That makes two of us," I said.

"I disapprove of medicines!"

"If you prefer to tell the court that the cause of your disgusting behavior was a displaced bone in the neck," I said, "by all means do. If you accept my story, you can have two psychiatrists, a pharmacologist, and an expert on human sexuality to back it."

"Bah!"

"And all will be well."

"What you mean by well?" said Otto.

I told him I meant a few weeks in my clinic on observation to make sure he was all right again, and I'd offer him reduced fees.

"Robbery!"

Prison, I continued, would be free, naturally. In the clinic I'd see he got plenty of cheese, and they didn't serve that to convicts.

"I tell them the truth!"

But I think he realized as he said it that cheese which had been poisoned with a new and unknown sex substance wouldn't go down very well against psychiatric testimony. After a long look at his toe, and waggling it about inside its sock, he said, "What must I do for this?"

"Hand over the marriage documents—all of them."

His face fell a yard. "I have no documents. It is bluff. We are not married."

I got up and went towards the bell push.

"Please! No! It was no marriage! I had a wife already!"

"Then I'll have that wedding certificate."

"It is in Hungary."

"I'll settle," I said, "for an affidavit that you've committed bigamy, to be drawn in terms which don't amount to an admission of a criminal offense."

He looked at me edgewise.

"If I'm insane, I cannot give the oath, huh? So your paper is no good?"

"Quite," I said, "so the choice is between unfortunate side effect and dirty old man. Which are you taking?"

Considering how he was placed, I came to respect Otto's bargaining stamina. After half an hour he had offered to play me for Dulcinea at poker or at chess, whichever I preferred. After another twenty minutes he'd suggested he should buy her off me against his next year's earnings, and that I should take him into partnership so that I could check them. It was only when the police sent to know if I could report on the accused's mental state yet that he saw the red light, and when I conceded, as I'd always intended to do, that any residence in the clinic should be free of all charge, we shook on it. The affidavit would be forthcoming (I had to trust him so far, but he for his part knew he'd be in my clinic, and I banked on his healthy respect for what our drugs could do to him). I had a tray with breakfast (no coffee) and some uncontaminated cheese sent down, ate a piece to reassure him, and left him to eat the rest. It occurred to me, as the door shut, that either he'd been really fond of Dulcinea to hold on so long in that situation, or he enjoyed bargaining and this was sheer needle.

I discharged him after three months. All the necessary documents had been signed. We even got the papers from Hungary, for I made him appoint me his trustee in lunacy. He seemed anxious to meet Dulcinea again, and she, for her part, fretted a little during his period of reclusion, but I was against a reunion. It seemed to me a case where a clean break was better. At the end of the legal proceedings I arranged his discharge and had him put on a train for Austria, still "cheese-excuse"ing under his breath, with a suitable gratuity in his pocket, cashable only in Vienna. He'd regained his spirits, and I felt sure he would fall on his feet, as well as making sure he never again trod on mine.

3
IN WHICH
ENGLAND EXPECTS

THE NEXT LANDMARK, ODDLY ENOUGH, WAS A SERmon.

Ever since that initial press conference, when we first poisoned the classes as a news story, I had taken the follow-up precaution of having as many BBC religious broadcasts as possible playing in our flat, from a loudspeaker in the hallway which was audible outside. Our own inner door wasn't quite soundproof, but as we were rarely awake on Sunday mornings, and if we were awake we were otherwise occupied, they didn't inconvenience us. I knew from experience that attention to detail is the secret of relations with the press, and I kept this arrangement going, with a time switch to control it, even after Gaudeamus's visit, and long after Dulcinea thought it pointless. On this Sunday morning, we were awake, however, and the door blew open, letting in the sounds of Divine worship. The rhythm of the first hymn was quite wrong and cut across any attempt at affection, and I already had the doorhandle in my hand to exclude it when I heard the voice of our old client Dr. Gaudeamus giving thanks for science in such heartfelt tones that I left it open; so that we both heard him expressing gratitude "for all those who plumb the mysteries of Thy universe, who listen to the voices of the stars in their courses, who unfold the wonderful workings of the body of man, and who by their study and counsel bring health, joy, and life into the homes of us all."

"We've done him a great deal of good," said Dulcinea, huskily, "and it's *lasted*."

The archbishop had obviously no ordinary congregation. After a minute or two I tumbled to the fact this was a service for the British Association Meetings. Granted the initial prayers were adapted to the use of scientists, from something in their tone, there was no doubt about the permanent impression we had made. In spite of the proximity of Dulcinea, I found myself waiting with real interest for the sermon.

And a cracking good sermon it was. I had every reason to think so, because I wrote it.

"The text is taken," said Gaudeamus "from Psalm CXXVIII, beginning at the second verse: 'For thou shalt eat the labour of thine hands: happy shalt thou be, and it shall be well with thee. Thy wife shall be a fruitful vine by the side of thine house: thy children like olive plants round about thy table.'

"Happiness is an attribute—which is only too rarely—associated in the popular mind—with the Faith by which we live. True, we all admit that there is in religion—an austere joy . . . ; and we would profess, no doubt, if we were to be pressed, that of course—happiness lies in the service of God. But that, if we are frank, we all, and those of us who are priests and ministers of the Christian faith most of all—recognize *that* is not the image we project. We may speak of the happiness which is in us through Christ—but only too often we lend substance to that old gibe of Macaulay's—that for the devout, bearbaiting is evil, not because it gives pain to the bear, but because it gives pleasure to the spectators. To say that pleasure, my friends, is not happiness, is perhaps the characteristic platitude of the pulpit. And if an archbishop announces himself about to preach on the subject of pleasure, many of you will know only too well what to expect. . . . I hope, however, that I may disappoint you."

All the time, with the dexterity of a juggler, he was playing a little game of pat-ball with the echo which came back from the walls of the building, breaking step with it whenever the cadence became soporific, and making his surprise points in phase with it, so that a standing wave jolted any particular section that looked inattentive.

". . . that the criticism leveled at us by the man in the street is still that which was put in more formal terms by Lecky—that asceticism has altered the proportion of the virtues, giving to chastity the primacy which in the New Testament is assigned to love; investing the devout life with a joylessness and a pursuit of suffering which, in the light of modern psychology, we know to be doubly unwholesome—casting a profound discredit upon the domestic virtues and upon sexuality, and dragging down the female sex into a deep and pervasive degradation. . . . As Dr. Henson has said, in common parlance asceticism is understood to mean not that reasonable self-control which is determined in the interest of nature, but an arbitrary suppression of properly natural instincts."

Little by little he rocked them asleep. Then, bang! by way of the marriage service, straight into Goggins, G. (1961) "A statistical estimate of the force of natural selection in determining different components of primate mating behavior." *J. Darwinism* 2, 148–83. "It might surprise many, as indeed it surprised me, to find that biologically speaking our service of marriage reverses the priorities when it sets the procreation of children as the first object, and mutual society and comfort as the third, which the human instincts consecrated in marriage have been formed to pursue." Without a jolt or a join he was off, abridging and improving my prose in places, putting in a word with longer vowels when he wanted a crack from his acoustic whip, crowning each of my piles of fact with a minute patch of uplift to tip the argument into line with his own assumptions. It was brilliant and judicious editing, a really professional job. Darwin and Freud, Lorenz and Tinbergen, Vatsyayana and Goggins passed in effortless procession and were blessed.

Once and once only did the structure slip—on the last straight, a few seconds from his final spurt, he suddenly took the bit between his teeth and bolted off the course with a longish sentence which wasn't in Goggins (1961) to the effect that who knew whether pleasure might not itself be a condition of fertility? The jolt was almost imperceptible, unless one had the text in front of one, but it was there; Dulcinea and I both exclaimed together, "Alice Edwina's pregnant." But Gaudeamus had already passed the post: "that synthesis of happiness and pleasure, science and faith, knowledge and humility, self-denial and self-realization, in which lies the true joy of Man's desiring. And now to scuffle scuttle stretch cough as is most justly Hymn No. 14 in 'Songs of Praise'—'We plough the fields and scatter The good seed on the land.' . . ."

And an audience of the astonished and edified devout and equally astonished and edified biologists bellowed the hymn and wondered what on earth Gaudeamus had eaten. Before he let them go, they had joined him in giving thanks, not only for sexual dimorphism and continuous polyestrus, but for those who by their studies and ministration were employing science to make matrimony more fruitful, harmonious, and generally interesting.

Dulcinea looked at me as if I'd somehow impersonated Gaudeamus in the pulpit and was bound to be found out.

"Chandra once said he thought you could sell boots to a fish, and I didn't believe him," she said.

"You can see now," I said, "why I wouldn't let Gaudeamus attend the classes." At the time, he'd been very keen to do so —I made the excuse, true enough as far as it went, that he'd certainly be recognized, and that if, as he wanted, he gave his real name it might embarrass other pupils. The real point, however, had been that his problem was an elementary one—he didn't need the full course, and I was very anxious to avoid exposing him to any of the medicated soap. Without it, we might have found that he stuck. On the other hand, I had a strong impression his religious vocation was absolutely sincere. If he'd been a worldly hypocrite, he'd have run no risk, but as it was there was a big danger that even a short exposure of 3-blindmycin would turn his episcopate into one of Chandra's puffs of irrelevance.

"And it would be unfair to him, as well as to us," I said, "if the archepiscopate were to slip through his fingers."

"It probably will in any case," said Dulcinea, "now you've been talking to him. He'll be ruined ecclesiastically because of us."

I told her I didn't see why. He was still perfectly sound. "He's got a first-rate mind, he approves of altar candles, he thinks nuclear weapons are a regrettable necessity, he doesn't approve of divorce, and he doesn't let moral problems rise above the navel—if we'd given him any 3-blindmycin we'd quite likely have turned him into a failure: as it is we carried out a conservative operation and it's been highly successful."

"Wouldn't he have been better off if we'd done more?"

"We had no real right," I said, "without asking him, and we couldn't ask him without telling him about the soap. He seems quite happy as archbishop. And what's more, he likes us."

The child was christened Sigmund George.

The sermon incident put us in mind that we were now free to marry—we'd been too busy to consider this, though I know it was never out of Dulcinea's mind for long, and we began to make arrangements. Some curious entrants were registering for the next course, however, and we had to devote a good deal of time to looking after them personally. The total intake was eighteen brace, but this included, contrary to policy and entirely by accident, two very persistent but unattached Americans. They came separately, but being of opposite sexes and both claiming to be called Doe we did not realize they were unconnected until we reached the stage of pair instruction, and by then it was too late to throw them out. The man was small, popeyed, anxious, and a graduate in English of the University of Wisconsin, whose life revolved round a publisher's advance which was to enable him to write the one millionth book about James Joyce. This was financing him in Paris. His story was that lack of sex experience made him unable to comprehend the deeper levels of *Finnegan's Wake*, but Dulcinea hit him off better than that. "I've christened him Lover Boy, for purposes of identification. And the other one's the Abominable Snowman—Lover Boy's mine, and the Snowman's yours."

The Snowman was another improbable entrant. From her external appearance she knew, or had once known, everything about sexual behavior except how to enjoy it with decent reticence. She was thirty-two by her passport (she kept the name covered) and looked older; she was a widow, and she was quite frankly taking a refresher course with a view to remarriage. The hat on top was easily mistaken for a coiffure which had miscarried, because it was covered with little rugwool tufts of an off-hair-color à la Masai with mud. Dulcinea, trying out her knowledge of elementary technique, was overwhelmed and almost strangled by beads. The voice was contralto but penetrating, so that there was never any doubt when Snowman was in the building. "In a state of excitement," Dulcinea reported, "she sounds *exactly* like a Russian locomotive." The class would then be kept waiting until the Snowman had remade her face with the contents of an aerosol can.

These two grotesques between them gave us more trouble than any previous members of the class had ever done. Neither of them could really be left to Ahmed or to Marousia. I could hear Dulcinea with the Snowman, "Not like that, it isn't a scrubbing brush!" and the Snowman's voice saying, "I have been married, you know, dear." Lover Boy was afraid of men like Ahmed because, he said, he doubted his own complete heterosexuality and might be attracted to them. The soap, so far from sorting him out, seemed to be making him miserable. He refused to talk to Chandra. The Snowman, by contrast, made a series of passes at Ahmed and was so jealous of Marousia that she bit her hand during a demonstration, and I had to be fetched to stop her sulking. They couldn't be ejected, however—I sensed that the Snowman at least would be able to neutralize the sense of our virtue I'd instilled into *Paris-Match*, and she was the story-giving type. Lover Boy was more like a potential suicide. Chandra, Dulcinea, and I all agreed that we were in real trouble, but there was nothing for it but to go ahead with them and hope for the best; this was so time-consuming that the much more important business of capitalizing Otto's documents and giving Dulcinea British citizenship, as well as making an honest woman of her, simply went by default—there was tacit agreement between us to finish the session first.

In addition to this, Marcel, Chandra, and I were slowly completing the paper which was to give 3-blindmycin to the world:

> Marcel, P., Goggins, C. G., and Ramagopala Tarunachandra (1962) Synthetic agents modifying human sexual behavior by the olfactory route. Part 1, chemistry; Part 2, effects on psychodynamics of the unconscious mind; Part 3, effects on overt sexual behavior; with a Note on their use in marital counseling.

We eventually decided on this form, rather than on three papers, Marcel, Tarunachandra, and Goggins; Goggins, Marcel, and Tarunachandra; and Tarunachandra, Goggins, and Marcel, i.e., a Latin square à l'Américaine, because of the need to get the whole thing out quickly without leakages from the editorial office. We had been working one evening on the final draft, passing it round for criticism—Marcel had left early (it was his turn with Minouche), Chandra had just followed him, and Dulcinea and I were washing cups before bed when the bell rang.

We had so few callers that I expected to find Marcel or Chandra back for something they'd dropped. Instead, the shadows outside the flat door contained the veiled figure of Horne Bros.

"Come in," I said—but there seemed to be something the matter with him. He had a mechanical, gooselike walk. His "good evening" had a tone appropriate to three matters only —funerals, public worship, and deep social deference. We sat him down. Something, I was sure, had gone badly wrong at home. I signaled to Dulcinea that this was going to be a consultation, and she began to disappear.

"No, no, please ask her to—ah—stay. I want to talk—ah— to you both, if you will allow me."

"I thought you'd probably rather see me first," I said.

"It's nothing whatever personal. Nothing of that kind at all—or rather—ah . . .?"

"Coffee?" said Dulcinea, gently, and handed it to him.

"Thank you—ah—Miss—Mrs.—*Madame*—ah—huh. One thing first. Can I assume that anything I say to you tonight will be treated as strictly and absolutely confidential—ah— between ourselves?"

"Unless it involves the commission of a moral or a statutory crime, yes," I said.

"And must not be communicated even to your professional collaborators. I'm terribly sorry, but it isn't my own proviso."

"If it doesn't directly concern their interests or their research, yes," I said, thinking about Marcel's chemicals.

"I think I must begin by saying that what I have to—say to you, to propose to you, that is, can't be said directly," Horne Bros. began. "I am an emissary, of course. I'm not in any way personally involved. Not personally. No question of shyness." He laughed, unaccompanied. "I think the reason for the obliquities in my message will become obvious as we go."

I inclined my head attentively and started guessing. "Now you know," said Horne Bros., "that traditionally the attitude to the family, the British attitude to the family, is a *way of life*. That is to say, it depends less on—what we say, what we believe than on *example*."

He looked me steadily in the eye. "I'm not of course talking here about my personal religious opinions. Treat me as if I were handing you a written message."

"Quite. You are repeating a message."

"Quite. Now that example is, of course, set by a relatively small number of—er—well-loved people whom we respect. Who are in the public eye. Who carry a proportionately heavy responsibility, which I must say they discharge unflinchingly."

Ye Gods and little fishes, I said to myself, it can't be! Gaudeamus, old chap, if this is a miracle I'll pay your canonization fees.

"And it is therefore a matter of very great concern to those who value the—family—that this example should be—er—unbroken. In fact, we have a very profound obligation to help those who set it. And if any of them should find that burden of example heavy—so heavy that being—er—human . . ."

". . . they look like dropping it smash on the toe of the establishment we should rally round and catch it before it hits the ground."

"That," said Horne Bros., "is roughly what I wanted to convey."

"So in practical terms?" I said.

"In practical terms, there are people—a relatively small number of people—whose marital stability and concern involve more than their own happiness. They involve the issue of *example:* in fact, there are those for whom discord is for that very reason unthinkable. You follow me?"

"And presumably some of those for whom it ought to be unthinkable are causing serious anxiety by thinking about it?"

"Precisely."

"And the sum of your message, if I can anticipate, is that it is thought, in the appropriate circles, that a few lessons from us might restore the moral Tower of Pisa to the perpendicular before it topples and someone is hurt. Before we go any further I've got two questions." Horne Bros. clapped his hand to his mouth like the third wise monkey. "It's all right," I said,

"I've got the drift of your message and I won't ask the particular questions you can't answer. I just want to know if the parties themselves have actually asked for our help, or whether it's being foisted on them by pressure from appropriate circles."

"They have specifically asked for it. This message comes from the parties in question."

"Good. Now for the second question. You'll realize that the help we have given to other people is the result of a carefully planned approach."

"I do."

"You can see that it must depend on the whole background of the patients and that we've got to plan our approach with care."

"Oh, obviously."

"And you know that social and quasi-social distinctions play a larger part in English society than in most others?"

"They are generally said to do so," said Horne Bros.

"So before I see anybody I've got to be in the picture. Agreed?"

"It's not for me to agree to anything of that kind," said Horne Bros. "It will be considered, of course, if you are willing to cooperate."

"I see your difficulty," I said, "but I can't improvise. Or prophesy. So before I know if I'm willing to cooperate I've got to know the social level at which I'm aiming."

"I can't say any more."

I passed him one of the little dummies we used for the class demonstrations.

"Here," I said, "is the body politic. Just point to the approximate level at which we shall be working."

"I'm afraid I don't quite follow you."

"It's presumably at some point between the crown and the heel. Give me a rough indication of the level."

"Very nice, *very* nice!" said Horne Bros., chuckling. "I'm most grateful for your tact. It's at—above the neck."

"A little more definitely?"

"It's certainly not at the crown, you can put that idea right out of your head. It's at the . . . level of the short hairs, I would say." He smiled weakly.

"Excellent. Now you tell me what you want me to do for them." And I let him recover his moral wind while I ran through the first few pages of Burke in my mind's eye.

"What I am bringing you," said Horne Bros., "is simply a private invitation." He ran a finger round inside his collar and switched to a natural tone of voice, like an announcer moving from royal funeral to football. "To spend a few days in England. You won't—possibly may not know your hosts, but they're—professional colleagues in a way. Lord and Lady Spadeadam—Vice-Patrons of the Marital Repairs Council—the so-called Glue and Plaster Boys. They'll give you a damn good time, so I'd accept if I were you. You'll be staying—I mean residing—in a grace and favor residence in Windsor Great Park. Quiet, I imagine, but plenty going on really. I'm sure you both need a holiday. Now—it won't be a big house party. Don't of course know who exactly will be there, but your fellow guests will include a young couple named Johnson."

"Original," whispered Dulcinea.

"The projected visit will be three weeks," said Horne Bros., "as the plan now stands. Do you think you can manage to get results in three weeks?"

"On the young couple called Johnson?"

Horne Bros. nodded reverently.

"You can have longer, of course. But then we'll have to break it up. They can't stay too long in one place. If you can do it in three weeks . . ."

"That depends," I said, "what the young couple called Johnson are quarreling about. For example, we can't cure alcoholism or broken hearts or even bad breath in three weeks —if at all."

"You may take it," said Horne Bros., emphatically, "that the only problem, in the expressed view of the persons themselves, is—ah—physical."

He could see I wasn't quite sold.

"Look, Dr. Goggins. I must press you. I want to know," he said, "whether you are on. I want to know now."

I made a show of weighing the issues. Dulcinea held her necklace and let her mouth go open a little way, and I saw her pick up her heel off the floor with that little thoroughbred trick. I brought her inside my arm, so as to associate us in the decision.

"In view of our impending marriage," I said, "I feel that we can't—let down the Christian ideal of monogamy, can we?"

Dulcinea choked and gave me a little slap, on Horne Bros.' blind side.

"In fact, we have an inescapable obligation to put those who set the nation's example, from which we shall so soon be beneficiaries, back in a sitting posture."

"That means?" said Horne Bros.

"We're on. With conditions."

"If they're reasonable. You know the form as well as I do. And of course *our* chief condition is absolute discretion. To which you'll both have to subscribe."

"This is the usual basis of medical relationships," I said. "All my patients can count on the same complete discretion."

"We would prefer you," said H.B., stonily, "in fact, we would *like* you, to incur a legal obligation."

I pointed out that I'd got one already and that Dulcinea was a qualified medical auxiliary.

"Er, no. In writing," said Horne Bros. "So that you're subject to the Official Secrets Act."

I pointed out that the provisions of the Official Secrets Act didn't depend on my voluntarily accepting them and that I regarded pledges of secrecy as unethical. Horne Bros. began to look really worried. However, I explained, I had no objection in view of the special circumstances to giving him a written statement that I would not divulge special professional confidences which I might receive between two specified dates, or any circumstances ancillary to them.

"I imagine," said Horne Bros., "that will be acceptable, if

after 'divulge' you'd be so kind as to add 'directly or indirectly' and after 'them' you'd add 'comma or by confirmation, denial, or ostentatious refusal of comment, lend color to any written, printed, pictorial, broadcast, or other matter whatsoever purporting to describe or comment on the confidences or circumstances aforesaid.' "

"I won't," I said, "but I will add after 'them' 'or assist any press speculation, or the like, on such matters'."

"I imagine," said Horne Bros., "that that will have to do."

Dulcinea opened the typewriter and went in search of a sheet of carbon paper. There was a pause in negotiations while she typed. I wondered if Horne Bros. had enough soul to notice a woman whose typing was castanets, and called up something beside office buildings, blotting pads, and weary virginity. But if he had he was too preoccupied just then to make use of it. The whirl of skirts as the roller threw out the finished document didn't touch him.

"Now about Divine Worship," said Horne Bros.

"I am a Śaiva Tantrist," I said, "of the Vāmacharya, or left-hand path. This lady's a Vaiṣṇava devotee of Kṛṣṇa."

"I know how you feel," said Horne Bros. "I'll try it for you, but I don't think they'll wear it. After all, you are supposed to be upholders of Christian matrimony in its most—ah—athletic form." I could see Dulcinea's eye signaling to me not to be funny about "athletic." "Ah—I mean you'll be watched on Sundays—it'll be *noticed*."

"By whom?"

He grinned wearily. "You know damned well by whom—do you really think I can list them? All your fellow guests will be observers on behalf ah—"

"Of the Larger Cats."

"Precisely."

I told him that I was not going to be sprayed weekly with moral disinfectant no matter who might be watching.

"It's *not* that at all," said H.B., "there's also the business of proving you aren't—ah—members of the Roman—ah—not wholly in sympathy—I mean, Goggins is presumably Geoghan, McGredy, Fuentes—it'll look bad."

"I will do my puja in Trafalgar Square," I said, "with full publicity. There were plenty of Hindus at the last Coronation —and Papists if it comes to that—and I didn't notice any objection."

"It isn't the *point*," said H.B., "in the position in which you'll be placed. . . . Oh well, I'll do my best for you. At least we can get you married. Or can't we?" He looked hard at me, then at Dulcinea.

"I'm a little surprised," I said, "that irregularity doesn't disqualify."

"Oh, no—irregularity in *itself* isn't a socially sensitive matter—I mean, it couldn't very well. What *is* a sensitive matter is whether you've ever been *divorced*."

"*I* haven't," said Dulcinea, brightly, "not once."

"Nor," I said, "have I."

Horne Bros.' face uncreased. He took a very deep breath.

"Then it looks," he said, "as if this is going to be all right."

I thought of Hillary a few feet from the top of Everest, battling with wind, cold, oxygen lack, and the deadline for Coronation Day. Horne Bros. was within reach of the pinnacle of his career, testing every handhold, putting his weight slowly on every step as he cut it. I almost regretted the anxiety my perversity must have caused him. Now his eye had the salmon's confidence, as it is hauled ashore, in its skill at catching Man.

"You haven't mentioned—remuneration," said Horne Bros. He spread "remuneration" like butter. I could see it dripping through toast as he pronounced the word.

"Need I mention it?"

"Oh no, no. You certainly needn't! You can assume . . ."

"I'm assuming standard clinic fees—that means twenty guineas per married couple per course." Dulcinea opened her mouth to speak, but didn't. "Unless the Johnsons are in receipt of Public Assistance. In that case I'd naturally waive—"

"They aren't. Well, not in the sense you mean. But Dr. Goggins, surely—"

"But obviously I shall have to ask them to find our travel and out-of-pocket expenses on the usual basis."

Horne Bros. gave a little bank-managerial chuckle. "You needn't worry. You needn't worry at all. But if you know your Bible, as no doubt you do, you'll remember the gentleman to whom it was said, 'Friend, come up higher.' This is good for what is colloquially known as a thou a day, and well you know it."

"Guineas?" I said.

"Well, naturally."

"I don't see any need to increase my fee above the normal twenty guineas, and a guinea for the groom!"

"*You* don't," said Horne Bros., "but *they* will. I mean, look, memoirs, old boy—*News of the World, Confidential, Paris-Match!* They won't obviously pay as much as the press boys, because as you very well know, this would be the next payoff story after the Flood and the Resurrection, but they'll insist on seeing you get enough to inculcate a sense of obligation . . . Yes, yes, I know about that written undertaking, but our experience is that without a stiffener—not getting at you, of course, but it's just the outcome of years and years of practical experience of human nature. Taking your offer would be, well, inexperienced. We may be ah—plodders—but we aren't *that*."

"I could give the balance away," I said.

"The more fool you, if I may say so."

"Half to the Rationalist Press Association, and half to the Irish Republican Army."

"I can't help it. No thou a day, no contract—those are my orders, anyhow—take it or leave it. Half of it's on the taxpayers. And of course, if you succeed, as I'm quite sure you will, there'll be less tangible but no less—ah—to most people—ah—welcome opportunities for the parties and—ah—others to indicate their gratitude."

"In plain?"

"Well, for a start you're booked in any case for an honorary degree each. That's not payment, it's been arranged as a cover story for your visit. Then . . ."

Unfortunately for the effect, he dropped the slip of paper he'd been palming, and furtively inspecting. I picked it up, and pretended he'd handed it to me to read. On it was penciled: "1000 min, insist. Keep under 3000 if poss. Firm offer if results— hon. deg., handshake, C.B. Dangle—F.R.S., ? N.Y. hons, (not O.M.; not kt—known to be radical). Don't overplay toff spiel."

"Very generous and very well judged," I said, and I handed him his shopping list back.

"Since you've seen it," said Horne Bros., "there's no more to say. Except that C.B. doesn't stand for Companion of the Bath."

"What does it stand for? It would be nice to know."

"Conveyor belt. Now you've had the lot."

"Subject to my fiancée's judgment," I said, "we are on."

"Do you mind if I phone?"

And he did.

The arrangements for my marriage to Dulcinea were made at the Embassy. Everything was converging to a finishing point and a sewing up of loose ends. We had the paper nearly ready: Chandra would be returning to India for three months' leave shortly before our English visit was due to begin—Ahmed and Marousia would work off the backlog of applicants, assisted by the sound-and-film teaching material which we had prepared, and the classes would then close until Chandra came back full time, with the wife he intended to marry meanwhile. Dulcinea and I would not return to Paris, but fly straight to India from London when our business in England was completed.

Horne Bros.' security arrangements were wasted, because both Chandra and Marcel immediately twigged the approximate purpose behind our alteration of plan, but they purposely said nothing and accepted my refusal to give them a forwarding address without comment. This was the best possible outcome, since I had to spend a good deal of time in comings and goings to visit Horne Bros.—my teaching material had to be sent by Diplomatic Bag to avoid seizure by the Customs, mattresses to my specification for mechanical properties had to be ordered, checked, and sent to be installed in the Spadeadam establishment (I was not risking the need to hunt round London while my charges were kept waiting), and an important document, agreeing that the content, manner, and methods of instruction to be given should rest at my sole discretion, subject to no inquiry, inspection, or interference by anyone whatsoever, had to be signed by a suitable plenipotentiary. The employers' side had its own condition: an emissary of Boyo's staff was to interview Dulcinea to produce the press cover story for her past life. A very pleasant young woman came and talked to her, and Dulcinea was disarmingly frank. The result was ready a few days later, when I left the classes for an afternoon to settle the wedding arrangements with Horne Bros. for the following Thursday. I'd vetoed an attempt to bring Dr. Gaudeamus over specially to marry us—it would only make us conspicuous and I thought it unfair to him, though I felt sure he would have come.

Horne Bros. gave me Dulcinea's new life story to read. It was a typical Boyo production:

> Mrs. Dulcinea Goggins was born in Buenos Aires, Argentina, of an old Anglo-Irish family on her father's side; her mother's family traces its European origin back to the Dukes of Alva. This ancestry alone might have been expected to prepare her for a life of adventure, but even so her storybook career would make many men of action envious. Educated first in South America, then in Britain, at St. Pinhilda's, Folkestone, she was completing her schooling with private tutors in Hungary when she was trapped there by the outbreak of war. She does not like to discuss the experiences first of Nazi and later of Communist occupation—she experienced privation, and was obliged to go into hiding more than once, but all the time she was pursuing a lifetime determination to give herself to medical and social work: she qualified the hard way,

becoming, during the years of Communist rule, assistant to a distinguished Hungarian physiotherapist, and it was with his assistance that she escaped after the failure of the 1958 Hungarian uprising first to Austria and later to France, where she met and married Dr. George Goggins, the leading marriage-guidance worker. It was a case of love at first sight, which extended to their professional interests, and together they developed the system of counseling which has made them celebrated in social science circles. It is as guests of the Marital Repairs Council that they are visiting England, before going on to India, where Dr. Goggins is in charge of medical research.

No additions without contacting Central Office of Information. Photo material—glossies or screen blocks available.

I had no chance to report this to Dulcinea, because when I reached the Clinic, Chandra was waiting for me. "Come in the office," he said, "it is serious." Then, when he'd shut the door, "We have solved the mystery of Lover Boy. The little worm is an American secret agent."

This had crossed my mind, though my money was actually on the Snowman.

"After what?" I asked him. "Or don't we know? If the President has a marital problem, refer him to the Vatican."

"Need you ask what he's after? Marcel could never keep his mouth shut."

"Did Lover Boy have a change of heart, or something?"

"Dulcinea got it out of him. When she paired him up with the Abominable Snowman again today he burst into tears, so she brought him in here and let him cry on her stomach, which was what he wanted. He was homesick and thoroughly maudlin, and he has talked and talked about his mother in Wisconsin, but he didn't come to the point. By her very truly remarkable intuition, your Dulcinea has guessed it, and asked him directly if he had anything he wanted to confess to her. Then out it all came; it was like turning on Dostoievsky's bath tap. Evidently his spying is motivated by a residue of infantile sexual curiosity. Three-blindmycin has removed this motivation, and Dulcinea has the transference. He has even given her his poison pin to look after."

"I expected something like this one day," I told him. "So long as cocuficin hasn't leaked, that's all. I'm not worried about the other things. They'll make a jollier sort of chemical warfare than most. Most Marxists of my acquaintance would be all the better for some 3-blindmycin."

"They want it," said Chandra, "not, as you might think, for the Russians. Believe it or not, it has been all the way up to the Vatican and down again, if he is speaking the truth. It has been ruled that the mass use of such agents is illicit and carries the condemnation of mortal sin, but that they may be employed sparingly to discredit individuals insufficiently enthusiastic about the Cold War under condemnation only of venial sin."

"Very jolly," I said. "We shall have to do something about it nevertheless."

"Dulcinea," said Chandra, "has already gained time. She has choked him off. She has told him that Marcel is deranged, which is true: that there is no such thing as 3-blindmycin, which is a pardonable falsehood, and that it is an easily recognized sexual delusion."

"Did he believe it?"

"He would believe anything said to him by Dulcinea. A little child could lead him provided it is a female child."

"Well, she showed great presence of mind," I said, "but it won't last. It's too easy. We need to move fast. Get Marcel here and warn him—ask the secretary at the hospital to start getting the paper ready for press. I'll deal with the laboratory."

Dulcinea appeared in the door. "Chandra's told you? It's pathetic," she said. I told her she had handled it magnificently.

"Here's his poison pin." She held it up. "Shall I put it down the toilet?"

"No. Give it to Marcel. He may well need it."

When it was dark I took Marcel back to the lab; the staff had left long since. Between us we removed all the 3-blindmycin and everything else to do with it, for transfer to Chandra's safe at the Indian Embassy, and replaced it with a full set of dummies—ampoules containing water with a dash of methylethyl pyridine for a smell, dummy notes, dummy experiments. No more real work was to be done in the department. Meanwhile we would get the paper off to press. Marcel was to go and see Francodor in three weeks, just as soon as we had gone.

In the event, we weren't a minute too soon. Lover Boy didn't reappear at the clinic, but the meter in Marcel's lab was read four times during the next week, and there were two batches of unsolicited and unpaid plumbers at work on his pipes. On the Friday, events took a more serious turn. Marcel had hailed a taxi which was not a taxi; which had been manifestly lying in wait for him—if he had not had a long piece of glass tubing inside his newspaper he would not have got out. As it was, he used this Marseilles-bottle-wise with remarkably good results and got the door open. In fact, he arrived at the clinic in a state of exaltation. "The blood," he said, "is theirs."

I told him that that wasn't the point. We held a council of war about the disposal of Marcel and decided the only thing to do was to follow up Dulcinea's original idea. Marcel had to be deranged. He could have a nervous breakdown. I would admit him to the clinic to prove it, put him in a side ward where the Communist Party had a sizable representation on the nursing staff, and tell them that the Americans were after him for left-wing militancy. That ought to ensure him a bodyguard.

Marcel was so recalcitrant about this proposal that Chandra and I had to threaten to certify him. He only agreed, reluctantly, when Minouche rang up in distraction to say that her flat had been burgled. As a concession, we put her on the nursing staff as an auxiliary, so that she could come in on Marcel's day in each week. She was to get the time off from the paint industry library by playing up the patriotic importance of nursing. "If she's in danger," I said, "she can come whole time and live in, and you'll have to give the rest of the shareholders their money back."

On the Thursday after, we were married. There was a touch of anticlimax about it—the Embassy staff did their best, Horne Bros. and Chandra were our witnesses, and there were even bridesmaids of a kind in the persons of Marousia and Minouche, but somehow it was a quieter wedding than most quiet weddings. The prevailing emotion was of relief, not exhilaration.

Horne Bros. pressed our hands in congratulation and told us not to bother about the certificate—he would see to that personally. We were to take the plane next afternoon. The flat seemed somehow unfriendly—we'd packed all but our immediate belongings, and Chandra came with us to start the business of seeing the crates on board ship. We'd already said good-bye to Marcel in hospital. I wasn't too happy about him—he seemed moody and almost as resentful as if I'd been in contact with cocuficin. I knew that Chandra had always been worried about Marcel's stability, and I hoped that when he came out in another fortnight he would stay on the rails. The big professional success assured him when our paper came out might help in that direction and restore his ego, and I was inclined to put his sulkiness down to the release of effort after all those years of work.

Our wedding night was restless, almost as restless as that fifth night together at Cannes, but it was the setting which was worrying Dulcinea—her conditioned response to rooms under covers, crates where there had been chairs, the tickets and the documents of travel. They revived all her past insecurities.

"It's happened so often to me," she said, in the dark.

"Never before with me. Never before with a genuine husband." She settled for a moment or two. Then she said, "George, did that man bring our marriage lines? He said he'd have them round here tonight."

I wished she hadn't noticed that little piece of byplay. I had. "I'm watching that," I said.

They hadn't arrived by breakfast, on the floor with milk

from the carton and the last cherry jam from the pot. Dulcinea said nothing, but I telephoned Horne Bros. as soon as I thought he'd be there.

He was not there—or he was not playing—but a girl with a golden voice, who acted as a barrier between his office and the importunate, told me he was seeing to it, and that she was sure it would reach us in England.

"I wonder if you'd mind making it clear to him," I said, "that we won't be leaving without it."

I left Dulcinea alone for a couple of hours while I returned to the clinic for a last check. It was deserted at this time, the flower vases empty, the cushions cold, and only the slight fragrance of the medicated soap to remind me of our triumphs there. On the desk were a few letters addressed to me. Three were bills, one was an application for the course, and the fourth a doctor's letter. It was signed Johannes R. Hartwigg, and it asked if I could help him by giving some heterosexual training to a certain John Fossil-Jones, who was struggling with a prolonged analysis and wanted, against the advice of his analyst, to undertake matrimony. I very much wished I could have accepted. As it was, I had to mark the letter "Refer to Dr. Tarunachandra." In any event, it made no odds. He or I—it would be 3-blindmycin that would restore this patient to membership of the human race, and the results of this would be much more important than the redirection of his aberrant inclinations.

Chandra was there when I reached the flat, but the certificate was not. I rang the Golden Voice to tell her we were unpacking. Dulcinea's face was that of a waif whose adoption has suddenly fallen through. I told her not to worry, and gave her something to do—I knew Horne Bros. and his friends better than she did, "and between us," I said, "we have them exactly where we want them." Clearly she wasn't reassured.

"This may be the one time you won't talk our way out," she said, but she made the preparations I directed.

They ran it pretty close. We had only forty-five minutes for the plane when the Golden Voice rang up to say that Horne Bros. was on the way. When he arrived he found us unpacked. If he hadn't, I think he was under instructions to stall. As it was, he handed over the certificate as if nothing had been said about it. I read the document from end to end, checked the ink, sealed it in an envelope which I handed to Dulcinea, and told her loudly to pack it. When Horne Bros. had gone down to fetch the chauffeur we put away the ostentatiously unpacked cases, which were Chandra's, and got the packed cases out of the linen cupboard. We took a farewell look at the room and went downstairs, Dulcinea suddenly getting closer to me than she'd ever done before in all our descents of that same dark, soup-scented well. The car door was open and Dulcinea got in.

There was to be one last crisis, however. I saw Ahmed arriving at the sprint and Marousia not far behind him.

"We must—ah . . ." said Horne Bros.

I told him that we'd take the next flight if need be.

Ahmed took a time to recover which almost reduced Horne Bros. to tears. Marousia was the quicker of the two.

"It's the Snowman. She is *Life* magazine. She admits to me very proud she is shadowing you to England. She says there is something of a fishy story you want to keep quiet. I don't know this . . ."

". . . but we are here to warn you," Ahmed finished.

"What's that he says?" said Horne Bros,. from the front seat.

"Lady journalist got in the class—she suspects something and she's shadowing us."

A big tear welled up in each of Horne Bros.' eyes and rolled down his cheek. Dulcinea tried to reach him to comfort him but couldn't. He roared like a three-year-old.

"Boo-ooh, hoo, hoo, hoo!"

"Ahmed," I said, "by the beard of the Prophet, *give her something else to write about!*"

I did not need to repeat the order to a man who had been the confidant of Chibouk. "Within the *law!*" I shouted after him. But he was gone.

All the way to the airport we comforted Horne Bros., and the maternal thing cured Dulcinea's worries completely. By the time we reached le Bourget he was calm and she was holding his hand, telling him stories about Hungary. We need not have hurried, because fog delayed our takeoff—all through the two extra hours we were obliged to wait, Horne Bros. sat by Dulcinea and let her show him pictures from the waiting-room magazines.

Finally I saw Ahmed at the barrier. He was composed and smart. Through the customs grill I asked him if he'd managed to think of anything.

"All is well."

"What have you arranged?"

"Only I give her a story. I send her to Geneva!"

I didn't like the look in Ahmed's eye. He was looking at me as if I were Chibouk.

"You haven't by any chance sold her to a brothel?"

"Oh, no, no, no. Where she will be treated very rich and appreciated. Where else but to my old Master and Commander of the Faithful? She is on her way now to Chibouk et-Twatt, God bless him, by railway parcel post. With your card, complimentary."

"Are you dead sure she's all right? Here they guillotine you."

"Now when I ask you did I ever asphyxiate a woman? I have marked her "livestock perishable," and Dr. Chandra's packing cases were eminently robust."

"Well, I suppose I owe you my thanks," I said.

He looked at his cuff.

"Thanks are unnecessary since I am here to serve you. Only five hundred francs string adhesive tape and labels, two thousand francs carriage."

"Take it from petty cash," I said, slipped Ahmed my address in a sealed envelope and went to put Horne Bros. out of his misery before our flight was called.

Coming into London, Horne Bros. was asleep, exhausted,

the unfinished supper in front of him. Dulcinea leaned over and secured his safety belt. Under us the necklaces of lights were so close that we could see the unsynchronized flashes of innumerable pedestrian crossings in a country pricked full of bright holes. I reminded Dulcinea that she was home. But she was tending Horne Bros., wiping the crumbs from his mouth and straightening his hair, and she missed the occasion.

We were escorted to the VIP lounge, introduced to the equivalent of the stationmaster, and given sherry while our bags were unpacked. The proceedings were surprisingly long. They weren't at all anxious for us to go—and the stationmaster, withdrawing, asked us to make ourselves comfortable while formalities were completed.

"What formalities?" I asked, "we're official guests."

"Just formalities."

Dulcinea's refugee nerve was raw again—Horne Bros. had gone off to some unspecified rendezvous.

"Quite calm," I said to her. "It's expected."

"What are we waiting for? Why are they keeping us?"

"Looking for their escaped hostage—your marriage certificate."

"Oh, my God! And you told me to pack it!"

"And Horne Bros. heard me."

"But I did—I did what you said."

"And I unpacked it. Your case contains Horne Bros.' envelope full of newspaper, and I put in a few unwrapped razor blades for good measure. Pity I hadn't any cocu . . . you know."

"But my . . ."

". . . certificate of seaworthiness is in Chandra's pocket on its way to meet us in Calcutta."

We were summoned, a fraction less cordially, I thought, than before. No inspection was made of our documents. Our luggage was brought in and passed, ostentatiously unopened. But I noticed three of the knot of dicks at the barrier who had adhesive strappings on their fingers.

A young man with RAF moustaches and a check jacket was waiting outside.

"Allow me," he said, "to introduce myself. My name is Spadeadam. My car's round there."

4
IN WHICH THE
COW JUMPS
OVER THE MOON

After our job was finished, there was silence in heaven for the space of three days. We made no attempt to estimate our results—medically, they had been completely satisfactory: socially, we could only wait and see. Wheels, we knew, were turning. The fourth morning's mailbag ended all doubt. The conveyor belt was in motion. Its generosity was as great as its displeasure is terrible. I called the contents of the envelopes, one by one, to Dulcinea across the breakfast table which Spadeadam and his lady had provided for us in considerate privacy: "The British Council; the Director of Schools Broadcasting; the Peanut Educational Network—*Panorama*—the Educational Press—the Editor of *The Times*—" A well-known series of instructional records, "Method Films, Limited—will you become Society consultant to a firm that sells Scotch—four more BBCs, one Talks Producer each from Home, Light and Network

Three, and they wonder if you'd consider a panel game—begging letter—Visual Aids and Textbooks of Australia—British Council again, your photo for Annigoni—*Fright* magazine: will you do them a series on etiquette in European society—they say twenty-four, and you can telephone it; that means they only want your name, so you won't have to do any actual writing: BBC—will I give the next Reith lectures . . ."

Spadeadam looked round the door. By now we regarded him as a member of the firm—he'd even pointed out the microphones the other "guests" had installed to spy on our undertaking in progress. "Can I come in? Well, you've made it," he said, "you've definitely made it. Congratulations. I knew when I saw that pile. And the *Radio Times* is on the phone this minute, to know if you've decided on the schools idea yet, because if it's on they'll have to start softening this week, and clear a splash space for the director-general's message announcing it the week after next."

Dulcinea was outwardly calm, but I could see from the size of her eyes that she was inwardly stunned.

"What," she said, "shall we say to them all?" And her face said At last, George Goggins, my love, you *have* bitten off more than we can chew . . .

"Tell them," I said, "that we are on. For any of these which aren't incompatible, or unethical, or commercial, and can be got through inside a fortnight. The schools programs are on film already—I thought we might need them. The rest we'll do from India. And refer the book requests to Jebb-Jollyboy Promotions Ltd.—they're my literary agents. . . ."

And so, in a fortnight of happy work, we set the Revolution on its way. In the *Radio Times*, the director-general's message was brought forward by a week. For the soften-up, they decided on crash tactics such as they'd once used to legalize gays, only bigger—every news bulletin dealt exclusively with human reproductive behavior and the clamant need of the teen-age generation—then they popped down the message on top and gave the public seven solid days of that. The director-general did his stuff admirably.

This series of programmes [ran the box in the middle of the front page] has not been undertaken without a great deal of thought and preparation. Since the idea was mooted two weeks ago, we have worked on the full knowledge that we were handling dynamite. Now that our work is completed, we expect controversy. Some viewers, we know, will find these programmes distasteful, disturbing, or both. Others will question whether the school is the place for this type of instruction, rather than the home or the consulting room. All these objections have been weighed in preparing the series, and we present it now in full confidence. We have had the advice throughout of the leading medical, psychological, and social authorities; of the Churches, and of representative parents and teachers. We believe that the result will most nearly meet the needs of present youth, the spouses and parents of tomorrow, and prepare them to enter married life with an advantage which our generation did not have. . . . The series will be introduced by His Grace the Archbishop of Canterbury and a consultant psychiatrist, and will conclude with a recorded postscript by H.R.H. The Duke of Orkney and Shetland. (Schools Programme, BBC Television, beginning Wednesday 22nd.)

A guidance pamphlet for teachers and parents, warning them what to expect, will shortly be available from BBC Publications, price 6d post free (no stamps) or from any Bookseller.

Boyo, I understand, ruined the irony of this by personally changing "weeks" into "years." He had a staff working shifts on the favorable editorial comment and the dummy correspondence from "Parent of 3 Daughters, Name Supplied" and "Woman Magistrate" expressing public agreement. What shook them all was that none of this obliquity was needed. The public took twenty-fours hours to realize that the bung was really out. After that their enthusiasm was spontaneous. Before the week was up, employers were in such a panic over impending absenteeism when the course went out that they were sneaking TV sets into the factories. Grumbling about the school-leaving age died like a swatted fly.

So far the Conveyor Belt, in expressing its gratitude, was only giving us opportunities it was bound to regret before long—some of its tokens of appreciation were going to be less to my taste. After a few days, in one of the lulls, Spadeadam waylaid me with an OHMS envelope containing two printed pamphlets. The blank covers carried nothing but the word "Confidential."

"Just have a look through these, will you?" he said. "You probably expect them. This one's the—ironmongery catalogue. You can opt for any one item that's marked with a pencil cross—it says what they all are. I'd have the K.C.V.O. if I were you—it's nonpolitical and a nice color. Then the CB are going to do you one night at the Palace—you're rated 'no personal contact,' that's usual for nonheads of States; you'd have got a second night as a rule, but they're redecorating and it's tight for a couple of weeks. These are the printed instructions for that. And I'm afraid I must ask to have both lots back when you've read them—they're not for the press, you see."

I thanked him very much indeed and handed him back the catalogue.

"What's this?"

"I won't need it. Thanks all the same."

"Oh Lord, you aren't refusing, are you?"

"Say 'decline' when you write," I said, "it sounds milder."

"The snag is," said Spadeadam, "that you've got a perfect right, and all that, but your wife's just accepted already."

"Accepted what?"

"Any Dame. She's not particular which. And it's subject to you picking a two-seater."

"Splendid," I said, "then make me Principal Boy."

"Are you quite sure? I mean, doesn't she . . . ?"

"Dulcinea," I said, "did this on purpose."

"Well," said Spadeadam, "I'll tell them you won't jump—but it's a pity. And I can't promise they'll agree to do one of you while the other just looks on. I wish you'd settle for armor—that would give you something each."

It took time to persuade him that I meant what I said and that he couldn't appeal to my better nature. To decorate Dulcinea, I explained, was the perfect solution—no refusal, to hurt anyone's feelings, no tomfool title to make me look ridiculous. I drew the analogy of a tiara—stunning on Dulcinea, and fulfilling a psychosymbolic function there; absurd and embarrassing on a fully equipped male.

"All right, all right! No knighthood in any circumstances," he said, when he could get a word in. "I'll tell them. She has her Dame and you stand there grinning like the full moon of May and give this woman away. As if I cared—honestly."

Dulcinea was inclined at first to be defiant, but that, so far as I was concerned, was that.

Spadeadam drove us up from Windsor to Oxford in his vintage Bentley—through a bright dewy morning that made the Thames Valley look extra and made Dulcinea appreciate her citizenship more than ever. She was chirping about the whole business like a child going to the seaside—I was resigned to the necessity of going through with it, maintaining meanwhile as much personal dignity as is compatible with an academic occasion and a degree one hasn't earned. The trunk was crammed with doctoral finery. Through the windows of the Comprehensive School drifted the sound of our own voices, as the first of our television lessons went out to a spellbound and critical audience.

On the further side of Henley we were overtaken by a large dark-blue bus, of the type that conveys policemen to rent riots, which disconcerted Spadeadam by its speed and inconsiderateness. On its side were the insignia of the Office of Works, and it carried adhesive paper batch numbers like a football special. It was almost empty, but I had a strong impression that of the few passengers one was Boyo. Spadeadam said something indistinct about it being the off season, or the damn thing would have standing passengers. In one way and another it confirmed my fears.

When we reached Oxford, they needed no confirmation. Outfall College, founded five years back in honor of Lord Outfall of Barking, lay across the former site of Christchurch

Meadows like a recumbent cow, and from the carillon in its two hundred foot tower amplified hymn tunes were already welcoming the guests. The Provost of Outfall was our host at the lodge for robing and sherry, and through a glass door, very like that of Boyo's Paris office, I saw the other honorary graduands. No amount of cigar smoke could veil the identity of Boyo or of ex-King Chibouk. Boyo saw me and winked solemnly—whether at me or at Dulcinea I couldn't tell.

In the middle of them all, beaming like a Buddha and making himself agreeable, was Cranium, the vice-chancellor. I knew him well. He'd often done odd vacation work for my tutor at Cambridge.

When the occasion offered I got round Chibouk, who didn't choose to notice me, and plucked Cranium's sleeve.

"Vice-Chancellor?"

"Ah, Goggins!" He leered at me. "You've sent us all back to school."

"Do you mind telling me," I said, "how . . . ?"

"You mean, these?" He lowered his voice. "A bit Hudibrastic, you think?"

"Well, I know you gave a degree to President Truman," I began.

"That was some time ago," said Cranium, wistfully. "They run a bus now. From NATO headquarters. You may have seen it. Only three in it today, but it holds thirty-two. Frankly, it wasn't my idea. We exchange them, you know. They all do it now. Except, I'm told, Cambridge, but you're always behind the *Zeitgeist*. I believe it's called a deal."

"With whom?"

'The Grants Committee. A new biology building. I don't entirely like it, I must own, but it's really temptingly cheap at the price. And we have safeguarded an active right of rejection—we rejected the ex-assistant commandant of Belsen. And the gentleman who killed Trotsky—I forget his name. The Foreign Office was very insistent. So you, as it were, were the lesser evils." He beamed like a lighthouse.

"Who's the missing graduand?" I asked.

Cranium looked at a typewritten slip in his sleeve.

"Albertus. He's a refugee, poor chap. Distinguished medical man in his own country."

All pity was now so choked with custom of fell deeds that it barely surprised me when, as we were marshaled into processional order, I found Albertus behind me, out of breath in a manner I recognized by sound alone. Dulcinea put her hand over her mouth in time to suppress a little scream. Albertus was Otto.

All the way through the streets I conversed with him over my shoulder, prison-exercise fashion, while Dulcinea gripped my hand hard inside our conjoined academic sleeves and stared straight ahead. Otto, for his part, bore no grudges.

"You bulgarize up all my practice in France," he said. "Last time I escape off tyranny, is no good—I bring *her* in the train. You pinch her; as for refugees, who is interested? Not bloody the Friworld who tell me I better come. So I escape again, better this time."

What Otto had actually done was to wait in Vienna until an unusually violent exchange of abuse was going on between East and West, and the Free World was clearly about to be caught with its pants down. For this, as he put it, he did not wait long. Then he got back as close to the frontier as possible without running any actual risk, fixed himself up with some mud and scratches, and staggered into an Austrian guard post in a state of exhaustion. The story he pitched to the Americans provided at least eight weeks' diversionary activity for the Free World at an awkward corner; Otto was carried round shoulder high and given papers, leapfrogging over about twenty thousand genuine refugees who didn't happen to be politically exploitable, and before they'd sucked him dry and dropped him he'd already fixed himself nicely. The doctorate was only part of the swag, but it was important. "Now soon I call myself Doctor without making gammon," he said. "I do not say 'of medicine,' only I write 'of laws' very small." There was no denying the ingenuity of this little scheme, and Otto's morals were no business of mine, but I couldn't help wishing some of the genuine refugees he'd leapfrogged had heard him describing it.

So we straggled on to the Sheldonian, a long procession of distinguished geriatric cases bringing up our rear with a rhythmic thumping of crutches and rubber-ended walking sticks. Hark, hark, I thought, the dogs do bark: some in Jags and some with bags and some with their trousers down: so two and two, save for Chibouk, who occupied two lanes, and looked in academic dress like a full-size buoy, we entered the building, and the gruesome comedy was enacted.

The Public Orator did his best with us. Collectively we were "a skull-splitting shower and a credit to the Free World. Doctissima turba, decusque communitatis civium liberorum." He called Boyo the distinguished inheritor of Marcus Antonius, which was bang on, and quite safe because even if Boyo had understood Latin he'd not have known enough about Marcus Antonius to spot the irony; he was charming to Dulcinea ("how well Science becomes a beautiful woman"): Albertus-Otto didn't do at all badly ("exile from his home but not from the community of the learned"), but he said several things about Chibouk which struck me as being in the poorest taste and spoiled quite a nice little compliment to me with a ghastly dog-Latin pun to the effect that I'd made sure that boredom didn't put out the torch of wedlock—"matrimonii ne taedam taedium exstinguat." It was an interesting observation, incidentally, that both Albertus-Otto and Dulcinea clearly understood spoken Latin. And there we were—Dulcinea, Laws: Chibouk, Divinity: Boyo, Litt.; Albertus, Laws: Goggins, Laws: Spadeadam, who'd got caught in the procession by mistake, and wasn't on the list, Music (there was a crisis here, because being one VIP in credit they were naturally a hood short, but a Doctor's hood [Music] was passed up from the floor and they did Spadeadam, protesting, *sotto voce*, that he was tone deaf and it was all a mistake, with that).

Chibouk ignored us all in a kingly sort of way, but he did

address one remark to me. As he passed the port he said in a very slow and deliberate English one memorized sentence. "We have enjoyed the woman, but found her eventually exhausting."

Dulcinea didn't want to meet Otto. I didn't want Boyo's congratulations. Lunch was distinctly trying, and they prolonged it into the afternoon by adjourning to the Senior Combination Room of Outfall College and forming a circle round Chibouk while he gave instruction in smoking a hubble-bubble. I edged Dulcinea toward the door. Passing Boyo, I heard a whisper, "We're putting absolute alcohol in his coffee—don't miss the fun, old boy." Albertus was asleep, and his tune had changed to "degrees-degrees."

Afternoon was drawing into evening, and outlying residents could still hear Spadeadam bellowing like a cow for its calf, as he quartered the towpaths around Oxford, "Dr. Goggins! Dr. *Goggins!*"

Dulcinea and I, rocking gently in a punt under the shelter of the riverside bushes, our Doctoral gowns spread over us, heard it too, but we did not feel called to hurry. One afternoon of undergraduate life, I considered was a very small concession for Dulcinea to ask of the Conveyor Belt, and I let her savor it to the full, before I pulled out the pole and propelled her back again to the distraught Spadeadam and our dinner engagement at the Palace.

After dinner, Spadeadam went over the routine for next day with us, excused himself, and wished us a good journey. The last thing he did was to hand me a letter from Marousia which almost spoiled my evening. The classes were doing well, but irrevocable disaster had overtaken Marcel. In fact, he was quite possibly dead by his own hand. It was a dreadful thing to have happened.

It appeared that as soon as he'd had the all clear, Marcel had gone round hotfoot to Francodor as arranged, to tell them he'd succeeded beyond their wildest dreams. But his triumph turned into nightmare. He'd arrived late as usual, he had been shown straight into a room containing a huge shiny table with bald heads laid out round it like plates. Now Marcel excited was always incoherent, as he'd been when he first met me. He found himself in front of a board meeting, telling them, when they could disentangle what he had to say, that he had discovered the universal aphrodisiac, that the American Secret Service had been chasing him to steal it, that he'd had to go into a mental hospital to get away from them. "But we put them off the scent. Now they don't believe it exists," he said, "but, naturally, it does!"

Then it dawned on him that the board didn't believe it either.

The bald heads swam in front of him.

"What exactly is this stuff?" said an English voice. It was a consulting chemist from Manchester who was an old enemy of Marcel's and had voted against his grant.

"It is a perfume," said Marcel, hoping to score off him.

"I mean, chemically. What's it called?"

Marcel said it was called 3-blindmycin. The English chemist sat up, shrugged, and slumped ostentatiously in his chair. "You know," Marcel continued, helpfully, "they all ran after the farmer's wife."

Nobody so much as smiled.

At this point, clearly, he should have produced the stuff, there and then, and put them down. But, horribly enough, he couldn't.

Marcel had apparently trusted nobody. The ampoules he gave Chandra for safekeeping had nothing in them but saline. He'd buried the entire world's supply of 3-blindmycin, all save the few units I had taken with me, under a tree in the Bois before he'd gone into the Clinic, marking the place with careful measurements from a large log. When he came out, someone had tidied up the log.

He dug up half the Bois—then the police arrived and wanted to know what he was burying. Marcel muttered something about truffles, and fled. When he came back, every log for miles had been moved, and there were large police foot-prints everywhere. He'd been back twice, but the ampoules were irrevocably lost. He thought of getting a dog to find it—and remembered that it repelled dogs. So he told his story to the board—the great discovery was buried in the Bois. Without waiting for any further evidence they told him that his services would no longer be required. By the time he got back to Paris they'd taken charge of the lab, and of the dummy ampoules and the notebook full of gibberish which I'd planted to be stolen by the Americans. That was the last straw—or the last but one. He seems to have kept his head for a while. Chandra was on the boat, with another dud ampoule; he couldn't contact me—but there was always the paper, which would vindicate him on our authority, and it ought to be arriving in proof any day. He had to wait, for we'd agreed to destroy the carbon copies, apart from two which Chandra and I had taken, in the interests of secrecy.

He'd only to survive until it was in print. When he got back to his flat, he seems to have encountered a final stroke of irony, beautifully timed by the President of the Immortals; he climbed the stairs just behind the postman, and was there to collect a fat registered letter from the *Quarterly Review of Chemical Communication Theory*. Almost weeping with relief, Marcel had sat down happily to start correcting. The proofs were nicely in time to save him. But the envelope didn't contain any proofs, only the manuscript back. With it was a letter saying that "the enclosed communication has not been considered yet, as it is not in the approved form. It should be retyped in triple instead of double spacing, concentrations should be given in molarity, not percentage, the abbreviation $CHCl_3$ should not be used for chloroform when this was cited as a solvent, and the references should give last as well as first page numbers." If he would kindly see to these points, they'd submit it to the next editorial board, in six months' time. As he turned it over, stunned, a penciled note fell out—left there in the office and certainly not meant for Marcel—"Dear Joe, More continental stuff. ? Bunk. Alan." Below which was penciled "Make this frog write it out properly before I read it."

At this point he cracked—for a week he worked on the revision. Then he had bought a registered envelope, posted the thing back in the approved form, and got drunk on his final banknote. After that he'd disappeared. Marousia had been all round—to Minouche, to Francodor, to the hospitals and lock-ups and morgues, but couldn't find out anything. She hoped the Free World hadn't got him. I thought he was more likely to be in the Seine. But there was nothing we could do except salute his memory—I had my hands full. His scientific reputation was quite safe, at least.

Apart from Marcel's calamity, life at the classes was continuing normally. The Abominable Snowman was back, creaking with free jewelry, and was splashing her abduction all over *Paris-Match*—she was as happy as an abominable sandboy and she'd quite forgotten us. Chibouk had found her quite a novel experience and given her a whale of a time, and Marousia reckoned we had done her a good turn professionally for which we ought to demand payment. The other interesting thing in her letter was that in the new sessional registrations they had had only two brace of Smiths, but there were nine and a half brace called Kuznetsov. Marousia didn't know yet if it meant anything, but there were also two ZIMs parked along with the Jaguars outside. From past experience she was going to keep a special eye on the odd Kuznetsov, and she commended herself humbly to me and to Dulcinea, to both of whom may Allah be merciful and obliterate our unbelief.

Dulcinea cried over Marcel, but she too was too busy and too full of the novelty of our situation to be sad for long. It was hard to treat even that catastrophe as real. After Spadeadam had gone, we settled down in opposite chairs and simply enjoyed the thing as it was. I insisted on early bed for both of us, but this meant a division of labor, for we had separate rooms —his and hers. I tried to explain that this was traditional. When she asked me how things were managed, in that case, I suggested that by custom the partners must agree to meet in the middle.

"What, on the floor?" she said. "There isn't even a couch in the dressing room. And the chairs have arms."

I didn't think we'd need to settle this as a problem in social anthropology. We were to be here for one night only, and the suite was infested with menservants and maidservants which made discretion essential.

"It's a pity," she said, as we kissed good-night: "I'd *like* to have been loved here."

But as a judicious-looking fellow popped in at that moment to say my bath was ready, and there were clearly eyes in every doorknob, she went quietly.

The bed was springy, but a bit convex. After our own Stradivarius in the flat it took me some time to get used to it. I'd barely settled when I heard someone moving. I waited to make a grab, but the intruder stubbed a toe with a little squeak which I recognized.

"They shouldn't have put us in different rooms," said Dulcinea. "I can't sleep. I can come in, can't I? There's room."

There wasn't, by unaffectionate standards, but I was naturally not going to complain of that.

She gave a big sigh, and I could feel her regulating the new, expensive hair-do so that it wouldn't get in my mouth. We interlocked. Presently, I felt her beginning to chuckle. The chuckling grew until it threatened to bring down the canopy.

"Funny?" I said.

"Yes, terribly funny. I never thought you'd do it. A poor little whore like me, tucked up in Buckingham Palace with an honorary degree. It's frightening, because I know something's bound to give way. But it's still awfully funny."

"You're not a poor little whore, you're a rich little wife, and tomorrow you'll be a Dame of the most worshipful order of something or other."

"Don't, or I'll become hysterical; you mustn't make me laugh any more."

That was how they found us next morning—unashamed.

"Well," said Dulcinea, brightly, "what does it feel like to be a life peer?"

"At least *you* don't have to look pleased," I said. "That I should have fallen for that trick! When I was three the dentist asked me to open my mouth because he wanted to look at my tooth. Before I could shut it, he extracted the tooth without an anaesthetic. I still think *that* was a dirty trick. So, with respect, is this—a fast one, unworthy of a gentleman. Coming on top of that barefaced fake photograph of the Gogginses leaving Divine Service at St. Pauls, it shakes my faith in human decency. It would have served them right if I'd kicked up a row there and then. It was only my medical sense of decorum that stopped me."

"And the fact that it was over before you realized what was happening," said Dulcinea. "Stop sulking. I think it was very kindly intended."

"Possibly. But it won't wash off, and I'm labeled—Bloody Crutworthy is my boon companion. Later on it'll be Boyo, and Fundament—the lot. At least I'm damned if I'll take an alias!"

"Nobody," said Dulcinea, "will ever get the chance to mistake you for an Establishment. You don't look the part. I'm just a little glad that they've outsmarted you. You can give the Establishment one point. And I'm Lady Goggins of Konarak."

"I suppose," I said, "you value that."

"So would you, if you'd been as insecure as I've been. Don't be bloody-minded. Come out. We've exactly half an hour before we need go for the plane and I'd like to see the grounds."

All round us the contents of thousands and thousands of tailors' windows spiraled and chattered. A wind from the tomb, a sartorial Last Trumpet, had blown through the cellars of Moss Bros. Like the skeletons of the danse macabre, the party worthies and the Tory councillors, the birchers and the bull-shiners, the takers-over, the suckers-up, the whippers-in, were moving across the lawns to form a vast bank, a Chesil Beach of dummies, winding away to the presentation point—overloud voices hushed in reverence, boss-class accents polished by self-esteem, they savored the thing as if it were turtle soup, under the eye of the astonished and obsequiously mocking waiters, the sole living things, other than the parkland birds, in the whole windblown assemblage.

Dulcinea did not see them as I did. Her eye was kindlier and less affected by experience. In it was the look which meant "If only we could get hold of all these, if only we could turn them into live people! Imagine, they were teen-agers once!" At the edge of the lily pond I looked down and saw myself in the water. My God, I thought, I'm one of them. Who put these clothes on me? My soul has been painlessly extracted.

"Dulcinea," I said, "don't let's wait. I can feel kapok and wire in my feet. They're mounting to my knees. If they reach much higher I shan't be able to walk. I shall have a polished boxwood knob where my head is. Don't let's risk it."

"I always thought," she said, "there was something aristo-cratic about you." She was reading that little inscription over my head. "I told the man we'd have Adam and Eve, proper, as supporters for our arms."

"Dulcinea, I think I'm going to be sick."

"You can't! My God, George, look!"

She suddenly sounded really frightened.

"What at?"

"That waiter. Watch when he turns round."

"There's something familiar," I said, "about the back."

"There certainly is."

He didn't turn round, and Dulcinea wouldn't explain. She put it down to the excitement, but my preconscious mind kept plucking my sleeve. We moved into the edge of the dummy-drift and it opened to salute us. Leading a reluctant Dulcinea, I made my way toward the exit.

"It's a pity to miss . . ."

"Dulcinea, I can stand no more."

A waiter was moving crabwise across our path, pushing through the guests in a way which struck me as unwaiterly. He was carrying a tray. Dulcinea seized my arm: the gait was familiar. The waiter was Marcel. He crossed our orbit, tray held out, and saw me—evidently he'd been quartering to find me. On the tray was a magnum, a magnum by itself—no ice, no cooler, no glasses. Its sides had been scored with a diamond after the fashion of a Molotov cocktail. As he passed me he tapped it. Insanity was in his eye. He disappeared into the thick of the drift and the dummies fell back into place behind him. He was gone.

Realization didn't dawn until he was out of sight.

"My God," I said to Dulcinea, *"there's a full quart in that bottle.* Enough to liberalize the superego of every man, woman, and child on the Earth's surface. We must stop him."

But he was nowhere to be seen. I'd have gone searching, but she put her hand on my arm. "You can't. I saw him slip down the service entrance. Beside—will it do any harm?"

"Look," I said, "let's get out of here before it happens. You don't understand. You don't know the full significance of our institutions. Ten thousand years of humbug are like gravity. You tense your muscles under it. This lot are shortly going to become weightless, and when the British ruling class loses its inhibitions I'm not stopping by. Run for it—*everybody out of this lab!"*

We were beginning to attract notice as I dragged her to the exit.

"My wrap!"

"No time," I said, pulling harder, "buy you another in Calcutta." I tripped over a peacock.

We passed the detective, the flunky swung open the gate, the policeman saluted. A voice offered to call us a taxi. We dived through the tourists goggling, and the traffic; only just in time. We were level with Queen Victoria, when I heard the first shout of surprise, even through the thickness of the building. It was followed by a series of screams. Policemen moved from a trot to a sprint, like dogs converging on a dogfight. Then above the sound of the traffic the screams were succeeded by a great spreading throaty chuckling that grew to a roar and was punctuated by whoops, like rocks thrown up from a volcano as it moves into full activity. The wind was blowing from the direction of Big Ben, and the palace lay to leeward of us, but as we ran and reached the beginning of the Mall, I caught the unmistakable warm scent of 3-blindmycin at a concentration I'd never dared to inhale, and the gentle, rising exhilaration. Over the palace, a pinkish mushroom cloud of vapor, covered with suggestive convexities, was expanding slowly into the sun, like Venus out of her shell. A bearskin sailed spinning up into the middle of it and fell back. We took hands as we ran.

"There must be somewhere . . ." gasped Dulcinea, over the rising clamor behind, "at the airport . . . even a bathroom . . . darling . . . let's hurry."

A flock of pigeons in the road ahead stopped feeding and began to display to each other.

"The ardha-lambitaka-bandha?" I gasped back. I saw her true beauty for the first time, naked through her presentation clothes, running down the Mall.

"Anything, but be quick! So very quick!"

The uproar grew and spread and widened behind and round us. Holding hands, we ran on toward the Admiralty Arch.